EMERGENCE

EMERGENCE

by

Marian McConnell

CAVE BOOKS
St. Louis, Missouri

Published by: CAVE BOOKS
756 Harvard Avenue
St. Louis, MO 63130

CAVE BOOKS is the publication affiliate
of The Cave Research Foundation, Inc.

Library of Congress Cataloging-in-Publication Data

McConnell, Marian, 1954-
    Emergence / Marian McConnell.
        p.   cm.
    ISBN 0-939748-48-7
    I. Title.
    PS3563. C3439E64   1999
    813' .54—dc21   99-20079
                                                 CIP

Printed in the United States of America

EMERGENCE

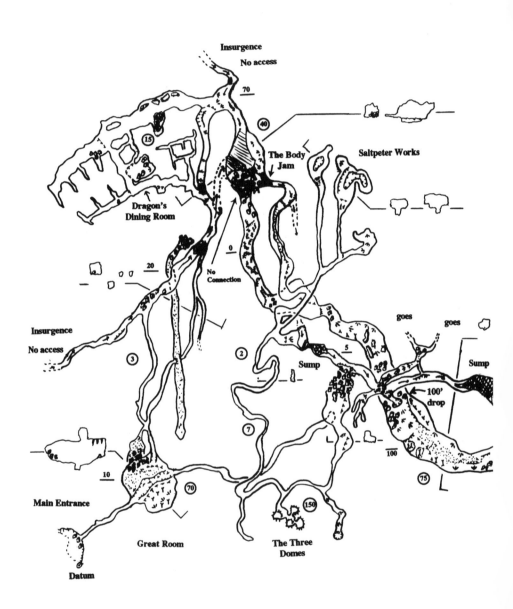

Dragon's Den Cave

Shenandoah County, Virginia

Tape and Compass Survey
by the Big Lick Grotto of the
National Speleological Society
October 23, 1994

Cartography by David (Hodag) Kuehls

Survey Team
Nicole Bryce
Joseph Coldwell
Dave Kuehls
Maria Kuehls
Max Stewart

Surveyed length
29,134 feet (5.20 miles)

Surveyed depth
185 feet

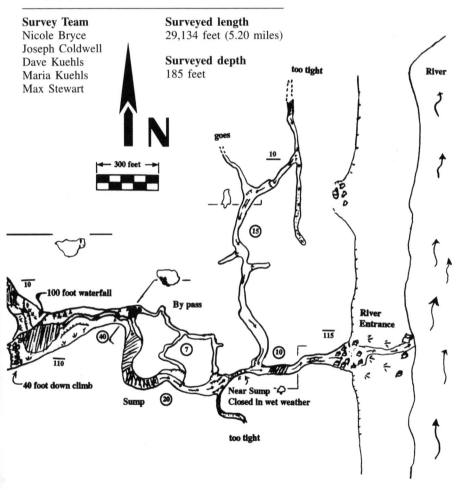

N

300 feet

too tight

River

goes

10

15

10

100 foot waterfall

By pass

River
Entrance

40

7

115

110

10

40 foot down climb

Sump   20

Near Sump
Closed in wet weather

too tight

Prologue

It was time to conserve light. The seven of them—six women and one young girl—huddled together for warmth and reassurance, then on the count of three they turned off their helmet lights. Darkness was immediate. Absolute. They strained to make out even the faintest shapes, but could see nothing but blackness. Their ears and noses and even the skin on their faces opened up to take in and interpret the sounds and scents surrounding them. Drip . . . drip . . . drip . . . clink . . . drip . . . a primitive melody played, and all around them was the smell of mud, rock, and clay.

1

Dancing in the Dragon

"Ready for adventure?" Danielle turned to face the passengers in the van as Nicole slid the side door firmly shut. She counted heads before pulling out of the parking lot. Besides her daughter, Kate, and the other trip leader, Nicole, there were four participants: Gabby, Sydney, Lynne, and Melissa. "We don't want to keep the troglobites waiting." Her face was deadpan, betrayed only by the mischievous light in her brown eyes.

"The troglo-who?" Gabby looked at the others for possible clues as she tried one last time to stuff a bulging knapsack under her seat. She kept her camera cradled in her lap.

"I thought we were going caving, not hunting for dinosaurs," Melissa said, wrapping a strip of leather around her waist-length hair.

Sydney tied a purple bat-print bandanna across her forehead, under a swinging ponytail. "A troglobite is a cave dweller, a creature that spends its whole life underground."

"Hold on ya'll, we'll be back by tomorrow night, won't we? I've only got a baby-sitter until then." Lynne waved good-bye through the van window to a carload of kids, three to be exact, plus the sitter, who had come to see her off. She felt deliciously guilty to be doing something on her own. Chuckling, she recalled the look on her kids' faces when she told them she was going to spend the night in a cave.

"Don't worry," Nicole said. "We're trogloxenes—cave visitors. We'll only be in the cave overnight. If we were troglobites, we'd be completely colorless, have blind eyes, and probably a couple of long, wiggly antennae."

"Sounds like my ex-boyfriend," muttered Lynne.

Everyone laughed. The trip had officially begun.

Caving and rock climbing had proven to be such excellent activities for building trust and self-confidence that they had become two of the main components of the Roanoke Parks & Recreation's outdoor adventure program. To Danielle and Nicole's delight, four women had enrolled this time. Over the past few weeks the students had worked on techniques at the indoor climbing wall. They had also learned how to rappel down and climb up a rope at Fools Face—a cliff near the New River. The overnight caving trip was to combine all they had learned in a fitting graduation adventure.

Kate, Danielle's daughter, a seasoned caver and climber at the tender age of eight, sat up straight in the window seat behind her mother. She kicked off her scuffed white tennis shoes (the second pair that month, she kept growing out of everything) and crossed her legs on the vinyl seat.

Danielle navigated the van down the interstate, happily fielding questions and comments from her passengers.

"Will I get claustrophobia?" Gabby asked, checking the lens of her camera for any dust or smudges.

"No, I don't think you'll have to worry about claustrophobia; this cave is pretty big, and we'll work with you on getting through any tight spots."

"How did you get into such an unusual sport in the first place?" Melissa pulled off her moccasins and stretched her legs.

"I don't think of caving as a sport. It's a way of life. Ask Kate, she's been doing this stuff since she was four years old."

"It's fun." Kate shrugged nonchalantly at the admiring comments from the others.

Words could never fully capture the wonder and accomplishment Danielle experienced in caves. Not that she couldn't talk all day about it. She pointed out the window at Virginia's ancient Appalachian Mountains. "Beautiful, aren't they? Well, there's a whole 'nother world beneath them. Once you've been there, you'll never see them the same way again. You'll see the magic inside. Caves are like jewels, gift-wrapped in green, like presents waiting to be opened."

"Ooh, I like presents!" Kate said.

"I heard that," Danielle laughed. She glanced in the rear view mirror, then checked her speed.

"Why do you like caves so much?" Gabby asked. As the van passed a woman hanging clothes out to dry, she squinted her right eye to take a mental picture, the white sheets flapping in the summer breeze contrasted nicely with the rock walls of the house.

"Well, caves are great inspiration for my art work; all the unusual textures and shapes. I'm glad you brought your camera, Gabby; you'll see what I mean. But I'm also hooked on teamwork and adventure. This will be an experience you'll never forget, that's for sure!"

Danielle nodded at her co-pilot, Nicole, who was sitting where Danielle usually did. Her husband, Max always drove on their trips; he was one of those people who get carsick as a passenger. It seemed a bit strange to be going without Max. Usually they led trips together, and had done it so many times it was like singing a familiar song in harmony.

"You'll do fine," Max had said earlier that Saturday morning as he kissed Danielle good-bye.

He'd been caving since the seventies, and had gotten her hooked when they met in 1990. Years ago, if anyone had told her she'd be climbing cliffs or exploring the underground, much less leading trips, she would have laughed in disbelief. She had hugged him back with fervor; his confidence in her was invigorating. "But I'd love to be a cricket on the wall," Max said, stroking his neatly trimmed beard thoughtfully. "In fact maybe I'll get a couple of folks from the Grotto to visit Dragons Den with me. I'd love to see you in action."

"Max, don't you dare come spying on us!"

"You'd never know we were there," he baited her.

"Don't you think I can lead this trip?" she asked, trying to read from his expression whether he was serious or just playing with her. She'd been so busy with preparations she hadn't had time to have doubts, but now they began to materialize. She suddenly felt the way she did just before putting the first brush stroke on a blank canvas. Was she getting in over her head?

"Sweetheart," Max said, "I have the utmost confidence in you; you're my star pupil. Your being worried is a good sign, it means you don't take your responsibilities lightly. You'll do fine."

Danielle parked the van on the field side of the rutted driveway. She'd obtained permission from the owner for access to the cave, as well as parking privileges. The women spilled out, eager to get moving after the two hour ride. Everyone geared up in helmets mounted with battery-powered lights, coveralls or old jackets and pants, kneepads, and sturdy high-topped lug-soled boots. Sleeping bags, ropes, water jugs, cooking equipment, and other supplies were divvied up. Personal packs had to be carried as well.

Tromping down the two-lane road, they joked about being "cave women," then paused for Gabby to take a group picture. Perspiration trickled down their necks and backs in the July heat. It seemed ridiculous to be layered up so much when it was 95°F, but it was 53°F in the cave year-round.

"Now before we climb up this steep trail, there are a couple of things you need to know," Danielle said. "Carry your gear with one hand free so you can keep contact with the ground at all times, like a tripod. We don't want anyone tumbling down and landing in the road, right? Also, there are lots of loose rocks, so if you knock something down, or drop something, yell 'Rock!' to warn everyone below you. The bigger it is, the louder you should yell. And, if someone above you yells 'Rock!' what should you do?"

"Run?" Gabby said, tucking her camera safely into her jacket.

"No, get 'small' under your helmet until all is clear," Danielle said. "And whatever you do, don't look up. Max and I were climbing Stone Mountain in North Carolina once when someone yelled 'Rock!' and it was a bunch of wild mountain goat turds."

"Maybe the goats were trying to tell you something," Melissa said, "like 'get off our mountain.'"

"Maybe," Danielle laughed, "They had us worried the way

6

they were looking at our ropes too. Especially the big black billy with a beard; I swear I saw him licking his lips." Danielle winked at Melissa. "Ready? Let's go."

They grabbed exposed tree roots in the nearly vertical path to climb up to the cave's entrance. The cool air drifting down the cliff beckoned. After a final check of their lights and one last quick pose in the sunshine for Gabby's camera, they slid on their bottoms into the darkness through a long narrow passage. The cave then opened up into the first large room.

"OK, find a place to sit," Danielle said when they reached Lecture Rock. "Then turn off your lights so your eyes have a chance to adjust." Formations gradually became visible in the faint light of the entrance hole up behind them, and seemed to glow as though lit from within.

"Safety first," said Danielle. "We stay together as a team at all times. Move as a unit, like we're a centipede instead of a bunch of ants. For you cave virgins—Lynne, Melissa, and Gabby—the National Speleological Society's motto is, 'Take nothing but pictures, leave nothing but footprints, kill nothing but time.' And I've left a 'call back' with Max, in case we need rescuing."

"Rescuing?" Gabby said, "Did you say 'rescuing?'"

"We leave a call back every time we go caving. He knows we're here in Dragons Den overnight, and if I don't call him by 5:00 p.m., he'll know something went wrong. It's just a safety precaution. Actually, I expect we'll be out of the cave by 2:00 Sunday afternoon."

"Cool! This is so cool!" Lynne said repeatedly after they turned their lights back on. She looked far too young to be the mother of three. Her wide brown eyes twinkled and dark blonde curls escaped from under her helmet. An endless supply of energy fueled her easy smiles.

"You know, I feel better about myself after a couple of times climbing and doing all this stuff with ya'll than after three years of professional counseling." She stared at the strange unfamiliar world around her. "Cool."

The immense room was the size of a large auditorium, shaped like a cardboard box that had been crumpled and then unfolded, leaving its walls as skewed and angular as a Picasso painting. On

7

the ceiling were rows of soda straws, thin tubes of calcite that were the beginnings of stalactites.

"Stalactites with a "c" hang tight to the ceiling, stalagmites with a "g" might make it up from the ground," Nicole said.

"And sometimes they join to form a column, or a 'mighty-tight,'" Danielle added.

The lights of seven helmets illuminated the brown and orange walls and cave decorations, revealing the cleaner white of the calcite where less careful visitors had not marred its beauty with muddy touches. Beneath some of the formations where the water dripped, rim pools had formed, walls of clay and calcite holding piecrust shaped pockets of water. Flowstone glistened on the walls in strange shapes, resembling mushrooms or parachutes frozen into stone.

"Gabby, quit taking so many pictures," Nicole said as another flash went off. "Save some film for the rest of the cave. You don't want to use up the whole roll the first ten minutes, do you? There's a lot more to see."

"This cave should have lots of interesting speleothems to photograph, Gabby. It's a solution cave," Sydney said. Sydney was a long-time caver from the TAG (Tennessee-Alabama-Georgia) area and knew a great deal about cave flora and fauna. Her experience in rappelling and ascending ropes and exploring caves was welcome on this trip. "It was sculpted by the slow dissolution of the limestone by water."

"How?" Gabby asked. She thought she might as well pick up some background facts for the captions of her pictures.

"Well, if you'll allow me to get a bit scientific, I can explain it to you."

"Do it," Danielle said.

"Actually, groundwater won't dissolve limestone very fast on its own," Sydney said. "It gets its secret ingredient when it goes through decaying plant and animal matter. Does anyone know what gas is formed by decomposing materials?"

"Do you mean the ground farts?" Kate asked, giggling.

"Sort of. The gas is carbon dioxide, which reacts with the water to form carbonic acid. You know how your stomach feels when you get indigestion? Like it's getting eaten away?" Sydney paused as Kate let out a mock groan. "The carbonic acid dissolves the limestone about twenty-five times faster than it would with just plain water. It seeps through tiny cracks and fissures, making them bigger, working its way down to the water table or an underground river. The river erodes down to even lower levels, leaving behind open passages and cave systems like the one we're in now."

"That's cool," Lynne said, "But what makes all the pretty formations?"

"We call them speleothems. When water drips from the ceiling and walls, it leaves behind a microscopic layer of calcite. All these fantastic formations you see were formed layer by layer. Many of them are tens of thousands of years old. It's hard to imagine how much time we're talking about here." Sydney's light moved along the wet walls until it stopped at a vertical crack that ran from the floor to the ceiling. "Some caves are also helped along by the shifting plates of the earth's upper crust. You know, earthquakes."

"Earthquakes?" Lynne said. "Not cool! I'm getting out of here." She rose abruptly, almost knocking Nicole over who reached up and pulled her back down.

"Easy," Danielle said. "We were in more danger out there driving down the highway than in here from an earthquake. Anyway, if it's your time to go, you're gonna go, even if you're sitting on the couch in your living room." In the back of her mind, she knew that the possibility was always there; the cave could collapse. There actually was a section of the cave that had been affected by an earthquake about thirty years ago. But danger, like discovery, is anywhere and everywhere. Everything worth doing requires some risk, and she was hoping that this was something each person on the trip would learn for herself.

"There are over three thousand wild caves in Virginia alone," Danielle continued. "Most of them are solution caves, of all shapes and sizes. But in other parts of the world there are sea caves, caused by waves, and beautiful glacial ice caves that really are dangerous. There are caves in volcanic lava, and caves sculpted by erosion from the wind. The cave we're in, Dragons Den, is what I call a friendly cave, just a nice limestone cave."

"Why is it called Dragons Den?" Melissa asked, zipping up her jacket. All those layers of clothes were starting to feel welcome

9

now. "Is there a dragon living in here?" She hummed a few notes of "Puff the Magic Dragon."

"There's no such thing as dragons," Kate said in her most grown-up, authoritative voice. But she sidled closer to her mother.

"I don't know," Danielle hedged. "There have been several rumors of . . ."

Whump! At that precise moment, Lynne's pack fell off a boulder and slammed to the floor, causing everyone to jump.

"Sheesh! Hold onto that thing, Lynne," Nicole laughed. "There's no dragon in here, except in your imaginations. The name comes from the shape of the cave itself." She tugged off one glove to pull a well-worn map out of her pack. "See? It kind of looks like a dragon, doesn't it? We can look at the map more later; right now we need to get going. Right, Danielle?"

"Right." Danielle got up and slung her pack over her shoulder, and the others followed suit. "Slow and low," she said as she took the lead.

This was not a commercial cave with handrails, stairs, and electric lighting, but rather a three-dimensional obstacle course demanding constant concentration and careful movements. They came to a five-foot drop and each helped the person behind her slide down. Then one by one they dropped to their knees and slid sideways underneath an enormous fallen column. They passed the packs and supplies along, moving slowly and methodically.

"What makes people do that?" Melissa said, shaking her head in disgust. They had come to a section of Dragons Den that had been badly vandalized. Names and dates were spray painted onto the walls, soda straws were snapped off, and stalactites broken short by souvenir seekers.

"I would like," Danielle said, gritting her teeth, "to tattoo the word 'jerk' on the forehead of any person caught defacing a cave. Let him live with it, the same way a cave has to."

"*Justitia omnibus*," Nicole added.

"Just what?" Kate asked.

"It's Latin, it means 'Justice for all.' If you want to work in the medical profession like I do, you have to learn Latin."

"OK," Kate said, "but it sounded like you were hoping someone would get hit by a bus."

10

They worked their way along the steep trail, crouching to keep their balance, each one spotting the person behind her. Nicole was the sweep person at the end of the line. She had more years of experience caving than Danielle, but preferred the role of second in command. It was enough to know that she could lead if she wanted to; besides, she wanted to give Danielle the opportunity to gain some experience. With the participants sandwiched between them, the leaders could keep the group safely supervised.

Nicole was a Physician's Assistant at a hospital in Roanoke. Slender, with short wispy dark hair, her delicate frame belied her strength. Her knowledge and medical skills were an asset on any caving trip, as was as her sense of humor. (She had gotten such a kick out of Danielle's letter requesting membership into the Grotto, "I enjoy caving because it is such a sensual experience. The sound your boots make in the sucking mud. The furtive movements in the dark.") According to Nicole, half the fun of caving was sharing jokes and stories over a Brushy Mountain vegetarian burger at Bogen's in Blacksburg after a rigorous day underground.

They came to the stream that flowed through the cave, and knee-walked one by one across a large tilted rock that lay cantilevered across the stream. Getting wet was to be avoided since the humidity in the cave was so high that wet clothes would almost never dry out, and cold damp clothing could quickly cause hypothermia. Another reason not to wade in the stream was that it would disturb the fish, crayfish, salamanders, and other more minute creatures that inhabited its dark waters and muddy banks.

"Take your packs off and push them in front of you, and push the other supply bags through too," Danielle instructed as she entered a small hole across from the stream. "The Birth Canal is a tight squeeze."

"Are ya'll sure my butt will fit through there?" Lynne stooped over to peer into the tunnel.

"It's easy," Kate bragged. She was four feet tall and weighed sixty-three pounds.

"Easy for you to say, pip-squeak," Danielle said. "Bigger butts than yours have made it. You'll be surprised at what you can fit through."

"Wait," Gabby said. "This will be a great shot." She focused her camera on Lynne who had dropped to her hands and knees to begin the crawl.

"No way. You're not taking a picture of my muddy butt," Lynne said as she sat back on her haunches.

"We call it a 'buddy mutt,'" Kate said.

"Oh come on. Your face won't be in the picture, so how will anyone even know it's you?" Gabby raised her camera, waiting.

"Well, all right. See ya'll on the other side." Lynne flopped to her belly and pushed her pack into the low, narrow passageway. The crawl was about twenty feet long and not too tight at first. She could lift her head up to see where she were going. But just before the end, it squeezed off forcing her to lay her head down and turn it sideways, take a deep breath, and push up and out with her toes.

"It's a girl," Danielle said, as Lynne's helmeted head appeared. "Congratulations. Now turn around and help Sydney with her pack."

One by one they came through the tunnel. Then it was Gabby's turn.

"I don't know about this," Gabby said as she looked into the muddy tube. What was this, a human playdough machine? Would she be crushed by the weight of the stone that encircled her with its constrictive walls?

"You're smaller than everyone that's been through so far, except Kate," Nicole said, "so I know you can do it."

"What if I get stuck?" Gabby said.

"You won't get stuck. But we won't force you to do it. Being afraid of the unknown is natural. It's called self-preservation. Nothing wrong with that. The key is to get in control of your feelings. Try it, and if you don't like it, back out. I'm right here. Go ahead, give it a shot. The others are waiting. They'll grab your pack for you."

Gabby began struggling her way through, but as she twisted her head to look forward, she saw the passage became even tighter. Panic rose in her voice, "I don't think I can do this, guys."

"You're doing fine," Sydney said. "Just keep coming toward me. Don't try to go so fast, you'll wear yourself out. Here, push me your pack. You're almost there."

"How in the world did you get through this," Gabby said with her mouth in the dirt. "Nope. I think I'd better back up."

"Stop a second," Danielle called into the tunnel. "Take a reading of your body. You can breathe, can't you? Quit trying to fight your way through. Move by inches, not by feet."

Gabby swallowed, took a breath, forced herself to concentrate, then slowly emerged with a grunt.

"You did it!"

As Gabby brushed the cave dirt from her front, she saw the glow of a helmet light above the Birth Canal.

"Wait a minute. What's that? Nicole? Hey, I can see your light. You mean I could have just climbed right over the top of this thing? Did you guys know that?"

Sydney handed Gabby her pack. "But it wouldn't have been half as much fun, would it? Aren't you glad you did it? That's the whole point. Doing things you never thought you'd be able to do."

Gabby grinned in spite of herself. She had to admit she did feel proud for not backing out. She pulled her camera from her pack and framed Nicole's face as she came out of the crawl.

They put their packs back on, gathered their gear, and continued to a duck walk, where the passage dipped beneath a low ceiling along the stream. They squatted low and waddled through grooves in the mud made by countless previous visitors and cavers.

"Watch your . . ."

Thunk!

". . . head!" Danielle said, as they came to an overhanging ledge. "Are you OK, Melissa?"

"I'm fine, it was just my helmet hitting a rock."

"Well, it's a tradition to say, 'Thank you helmet' every time that happens. Sort of makes you appreciate the fact that you're wearing a 'brain bucket,' and it also alerts the people behind you there's something to watch out for."

"Thank you helmet," Melissa said loudly, now alert for any other unexpected protrusions.

The women continued onward through more passages, climbing and sliding, crawling and bending, stooping and twisting through the innards of Dragons Den. By the time they reached the Dragon's Dining Room where they were stashing their overnight gear, they were ready for a rest and lunch.

13

The Dining Room was spacious and round, with the stream encircling a relatively flat, smooth area on three sides. The ceiling curved upward and they could see swirls and alcoves in its high vaulted dome, remnants of long ago floods. In one area, an ancient stream had sculpted a huge cleft in the wall that some said resembled a dove of peace with wings outstretched.

"Looks to me more like an inside view of a woman's reproductive organs complete with fallopian tubes," Nicole said.

"Gross," Kate said.

"Gross? Do you know what fallopian tubes are?"

"Yeah, yeah, my mom told me all about that stuff. I'm only eight, give me a break."

Each woman's moist breath rose in the humid air and floated before her in a little mist. Gabby was learning that she had to hold her breath each time she took a picture, otherwise her breath-cloud got in the way. Her fascination with this utterly new and different environment overrode her apprehension, and she was taking pictures with abandon. The variety of textures and shapes was infinite; just changing her viewpoint created whole new scenes. One line of rocks made her think of hobbit homes; a sculpted boulder near the creek looked like a renaissance castle. And that odd shaped flowstone was a mischievous gnome hiding behind a flowing beard.

As well as possessing an eye for the unique and unusual, Gabby had that rare talent of making friends instantaneously. She fantasized about living like her heroine, "Sissy Hankshaw" from Tom Robbins' novel, Even Cowgirls Get the Blues, hitchhiking her way around the universe, thumbing her way in and out of adventures and romance. Life was to be sampled and savored. Taking pictures was one way of capturing it all and making it last. Now that she was a married woman with a nine-year-old son, she couldn't travel as much. So when wanderlust tugged at her sleeve, she could at least pull out her photo albums and relive some of those moments of freedom and discovery.

She tried to take candid shots of the others, but the stark flare of the flash gave her away. She didn't want to end up with her subjects looking like deer surprised by headlights on a dark country road, so she finally gave them a few seconds' warning and was able to arrange some fairly natural group and individual poses. Kate started out being camera shy, then made goofy faces, causing Danielle to frown one moment then smile benevolently for Gabby the next.

Gabby knelt to take a close-up of the packs that were resting together like fat little animals on top of a big flat boulder. Then down to the stream where a small perfect rim pool was reflecting delicate, white helectites, and soda straws. A sudden wriggling movement caught her eye and she drew a sharp breath at the sight of a fluorescent orange and black cave salamander. It froze as if to pose boldly, then squirmed into a niche at the shutter's click. Gabby patted the camera approvingly, "Good one."

After they had set up base camp for what they jokingly called their underground pajama party, Danielle gathered the group together. "Grab your packs, the ropes, and your vertical gear. We're going to head up the Breakdown for the Body Jam."

"Breakdown? Body jam? Sounds like we're going dancing or something." Melissa beat a jaunty rhythm on her pack, and hopped lightly from one foot to the other.

Danielle paused and adjusted her helmet strap. "Actually, caving is sort of like a dance. Haven't you noticed that you use your whole body while you're moving through the cave? If you go slowly and deliberately, each move is like a dance in slow motion. Rock climbing is like that too—ballet on the rocks."

Kate stopped and did an exaggerated pirouette, then curtsied to the glove-muffled applause of the group.

"Why do we have to take our packs with us? We're coming back here to spend the night, aren't we?" Gabby rubbed her shoulders, sore from lugging her portion of their overnight supplies.

"Your pack is your life support—like scuba tanks if you're diving. Remember the Scout motto of 'Be Prepared?' Well, you always need to have twenty-four hours worth of food and emergency supplies with you." After Danielle counted out enough powerbars and batteries to complete her own pack, she and Nicole checked the other packs to make sure they were well stocked.

"Some of the Grotto members have a nice way of teaching this lesson if you leave your pack behind," Nicole said. "They stuff

15

rocks in it while you're not looking. You'd be surprised how many folks have lugged around an extra five or ten pounds before realizing they've been had."

"We were caving in Tennessee's Jaguar Cave once during the summer and got hit by some torrential downpours that flooded the river and the entrance to the cave," Sydney said as they headed toward the Breakdown. "The cave was high enough inside that we were safe, but we had to wait an extra day for the river to drop so we could get out. It made me thankful I had so much food and water with me. You won't hear me complaining about carrying my pack."

They stopped for a moment at the bottom of the Breakdown, a spot in the cave where a layer of ceiling had collapsed sometime in the very distant past. Rather than think of this collapse as something to fear, Danielle liked to think of it as a talisman for warding off any more collapses for a while. Boulders of all shapes and sizes were piled up halfway to the ceiling, leaving gaping holes and slippery surfaces.

"Watch your step," Danielle said. "Look out for loose rocks and crevices. You don't want to break your leg."

Only a few weeks before, Max and Danielle had been leading a group out through a portion of the breakdown called the Screwhole. It was a narrow vertical shaft that connected the lower passage to the top of the jumble of breakdown. To climb up from below, each person had to grab the top of a large boulder wedged between some other rocks, and pull up onto it to reach the next hold. Danielle had already climbed up and was helping the others do the same when she saw the chockstone move slightly under the weight of one of the cavers.

"I don't like the looks of that rock," she said to Max, who was standing directly beneath it, spotting each person as they stemmed the dicey chimney.

Max made sure everyone was clear of the dubious boulder then climbed lightly over it. Turning around and bracing himself, he gave the rock some forceful kicks and with deafening thunder it crashed to the floor, taking parts of the wall with it.

They would take a different way now, via the Body Jam. This was a wedge-shaped crevice between the wall of the cave and a massive boulder. You negotiated it by lowering yourself vertically, your stomach against the boulder's sheer face, and jamming your body into the tight part of the wedge. Then you could slowly make your way down to the floor of the cave using your body's friction in the crack to slow your descent. There were footholds underneath toward the bottom of the twelve-foot cliff. Danielle paused, then slowly lowered herself into the wedge. "Easy," she thought, "just go down the rock, slow, stay in tight against it, feel for the ledge with your feet." The toe of her boot landed solidly on the ledge.

"OK, who's next?" she said. "You need to take your packs off for this. Nicole can hand them down once everyone's on the bottom. C'mon, Melissa. You like climbing so you can do this, no sweat."

After everyone had safely jammed down the crack, they paused to admire the slanted ceiling that marked the Salem fault line. An earth tremor countless ages ago had shifted the plates of rock and caused the ceiling to be lopsided along this part of the passage. The path got more slippery as they moved deeper into the earth and closer to the stream. In single file they slid down muddy banks and followed deep grooves worn into the clay by past cavers. Some footprints had become such deep holes that they were called elephant tracks. In a few places, they crossed the creek to the upper ledges to stay out of the water. It was slow going but they were having fun and talked all the time.

Each section of the cave had its own personality. One side-room was dry and sandy, a good source historically for saltpeter, used during the Civil War to make gunpowder. Hunters of saltpeter detected it by scooping up a handful and holding a flame to it as they let it dribble through their fingers. If the dusty particles "sparked" at the flame's touch, they knew they had found saltpeter.

Melissa told them that Indians sometimes used caves as a source of gypsum for making ceremonial paints. In yet another passage Sydney found evidence of the cave's underwater origins of long ago—in the ceiling were seashell fossils embedded in the limestone slabs, which were like great stone pages out of the cave's prehistoric diary.

Then there was the hibernaculum—where bats hibernated during the winter.

"Bats are so neat," Sydney said. "I'm glad it's summertime so we don't have to worry about waking them up."

"Why can't you wake them up?" Gabby asked, holding her camera ready in case she saw one of these peculiar creatures. "Will they hurt you?"

"No. But it might hurt them, and possibly mean their death if you wake them up too many times during winter months. Bats eat flying insects and store up fat in their bodies to survive on when it's time to hibernate. If you make a lot of noise or wake them up, they'll fly around looking for another perch, but without any insects for them to eat they'll use up energy they need to get through the winter. Bats are great to have around; they really keep the insect population down. But they're sensitive and need their privacy."

"They aren't the only ones," Lynne said.

Sydney stood still and scanned the ceiling, then pointed to a little brown pipestrelle sleeping silently in the folds of a drapery formation.

"Are there many bats in your cave, Danielle?" Sydney asked, tucking a stray wisp of light brown hair up under her "batdanna" with a muddy glove.

"Your cave?" Gabby said. "You own a cave?"

"It's called the 'Murder Hole,'" Kate said, always eager to talk about something that made grown-up eyes widen.

"I'll have to tell you the story about Murder Hole some time; it's a famous, and in some ways infamous cave in Catawba Valley," Danielle said.

"Can we come see it?" Gabby asked, taking one more picture of the bat.

"Sure, as long as Max or I are with you. It suffered quite a bit of vandalism before we bought it, so we're very protective of it. It's also a very technical vertical cave with three long rappels. If you do well today on this drop, you'll be able to handle the ones in Murder Hole."

When they reached the pit, Danielle and Nicole set up the anchor system to hold the ropes that dropped a hundred feet down to the lower level. The women took turns looking into the void. Excitement was high. The drop was completely free; each person

18

would descend, hanging solely on a 7/16 inch length of static kernmantle nylon rope. The hole was just wide enough to rig two ropes. If someone got in a predicament or froze up, Danielle or Nicole could go down on the second rope to assist. Two ropes would also make the ascents go more quickly when they returned to base camp that evening.

They used plenty of edge protection—rectangles of old carpet placed between the rope and the rock ledge. Rock can eat through an unprotected rope very rapidly with the weight and friction of a climber on it. Danielle stood back and ran through every possible scenario in her mind, checking her system to make sure each section had a back-up. If one knot failed, or one part of the anchor came loose, another would hold. The anchor was fine. She had used figure eight and butterfly knots, connected with locking carabiners.

"I like carabiners because they start with 'care' and they help take care of you," Kate said. Carabiners are steel, aluminum, or alloy links in various sizes, commonly about five inches long with either a locking or non-locking gate. Locking carabiners are mandatory when used as life-safety devices, which was certainly the case here. Danielle was comforted by the metallic "ting" as a carabiner snapped shut, and she screwed down the sleeve to lock it.

"OK, folks, first check your harness. Make sure it's snug and that the waist belt is threaded back through the buckle to lock it." Danielle checked each woman's harness. "I'm going to go down first and I'll belay each one of you," she said. "Nicole will come down last so she can help you get over the edge if you need it. I know it will seem a little hairy, but just remember what you learned during our practice sessions. Go slow and concentrate and you'll do fine. We've got a safety line to clip into before you even get on rope. Hang your pack down low so it won't get in the way or throw you off balance. Nicole will double-check to make sure everything's OK."

"Mom, can I come down after you?"

"Yes, Kate, I want you to. You'll like this rappel, it's nice and long, just the way you like 'em. Any questions?"

"Yeah . . . where's the Ladies' Room?" blurted Gabby.

The group broke out in relieved laughter.

19

"It's in your pack," replied Sydney, "It's called a widdle bottle."

"Well I'm a widdle nervous," Gabby said. "Are you sure I can do this?"

"Hey, I'm shakin' too," Lynne said. "It's a long way down."

"You'll be fine," Melissa said. "It looks like fun."

"You're just braver than we are," Gabby said.

"You're all brave," Nicole said. "It's taken gumption just to come this far and you don't have to do this part if you don't want to. But it has to be a group decision. We all go, or all stay. C'mon. *Fortes fortuna juvat*—Fortune favors the brave. How do you like that one, Kate? And just think of the beautiful waterfall down below, Gabby. What a photo opportunity!"

Danielle hooked into the safety line, then straddled the hole with her back to one ledge and feet against the opposite ledge. "On rope," she said as she pulled up enough rope—their lifeline—to lay down the middle of her mini-rack, snapping each bar into place in the proper sequence.

Making sure her ascending gear was within easy reach just in case she had to abort the rappel, she looked down again and made sure her carabiner was locked, that the rack was loaded properly, and her helmet was snug. She winked at Gabby who was taking her picture. She caught Kate's eyes and said, "See you on the bottom. Be careful. On rappel!"

She lowered herself slowly until her weight was completely on the rope. This was the part that always made her hands sweat and her throat go dry. Trusting her life to a mere strand of rope. Dangling in a black space and feeling suddenly tiny and immense at the same time. Life zoomed into focus as the lights on the helmets of the women above spiraled and the darkness of the vast depths below engulfed her. She pushed aside childhood memories from scary movies on TV, giant ants that lived in the sewer, and shadowy creatures appearing out of the night mist. "Whee!" she yelled as she dropped down the rope.

She wanted it to last forever. She felt free and light and amazed at all she had done and all she was yet to become. The solitary light of her helmet illuminated pristine formations and the floor of the great room was now visible. Not a monster in sight.

Reluctantly, (rappels were always over too soon), Danielle removed her rack and shouted, "Off rope!" to the women far above her. She set her pack aside and gripped the bottom of the rope to belay Kate. Kate descended using a rescue eight with ears instead of a rack. She was so light it was easier to use, and she had her own eight that she'd been using for years. Danielle admired Kate, both as a daughter and as a truly unique and special person. She wondered what Kate would be doing when she was forty, with so many experiences behind her already.

Sydney was next, slow and steady, with much confidence and poise. Melissa came down cautiously at first, then picked up speed toward the bottom. Danielle braced, ready to belay her to a stop but Melissa easily controlled her drop and touched down as lightly as a dancer. The room was coming alive with the arrival of each woman. Danielle had to shush everyone to concentrate on Lynne who was getting on the rope up at the top. She could faintly hear Nicole's measured instructions and Lynne's nervous giggles. She knew exactly how Lynne felt. Finally she could see the light of Lynne's helmet announcing that she had begun her trip downward.

"Wow! Cool! Oh my God!"

The group below cheered as their helmet beams flashed up to illuminate Lynne.

"This is great!" she said. "My kids would love it."

After landing, Lynne could barely contain her excitement and Danielle hugged her proudly. "You did it. That was cool all right. You did great."

"I wish I could zip back up and tell Gabby how easy it was. She's not so sure she can do it," Lynne said.

"Nicole'll give her moral support. Look, here she comes now."

Gabby surprised them all. She didn't hesitate; she came down the rope as if she did it every day, even pausing to take a picture on the way down. "Yeeha!" she whooped as she touched bottom.

2

Hard Rock

Shards of crystalline calcite shattered and scattered across the floor as BJ forced his way through the tight passage. He shook some fragments out of his thatch of red hair and brusquely rubbed the top of his head. Damn stuff's even falling down my shirt. Get your asses up here," he yelled back to Jake and Tim. He pushed ahead, barely missing another cluster of delicate soda straws. "It's about damn time," he muttered as the tunnel opened up into a room large enough to accommodate his wiry frame. His sinewed arms snaked out of a muddy T-shirt as he stretched out cramped muscles and then felt his head for blood. Just a lump. A flashlight clattered to the rocks from his back pocket.

Jake scrambled out of the tunnel to pick up the light, then laughed nervously when it blinked on.

"Here man, you'd better hang on to this." He belched, tasting beer, and tossed the light back to BJ. He hopped back and forth from one muddy foot to the other in a jig to warm his chilled bones.

BJ caught the flashlight, twirling it like a gunslinger, but as he turned to continue their foray, he failed to notice a foot-long soda-straw clinging to the ceiling behind him. One second it was there, glistening in the dim beam of Tim's flashlight. The next it lay in pieces at their feet.

"Watch what you're doing," Tim said. He bent down to collect some of the remains, studying them and wishing he hadn't seen the pretty thing ruined.

BJ swayed slightly. "So? No big deal. Here man, why don't you take this one home as a souvenir of your first cave trip? Chicks'll go crazy when they see it sitting on your coffee-table; you'll have to beat 'em off." He kicked at a foot-high phallic-shaped stalagmite until it broke off and rolled to rest at Tim's feet.

Tim picked it up. The world seemed bent on falling apart around him, one way or another. He turned it slowly in his hands, then tried to wipe away some of the mud from its cold, milky white surface.

Tim was a DJ for the local country music station. He had the kind of voice that made his listeners feel he was talking personally to them; this, coupled with dreamy blue eyes and long shaggy brown hair topping off a lean, athletic body made him popular in the valley's party scene. But two-stepping from one hopeful husband-seeker to another got old fast. He had enrolled in an evening computer class that gave him a socially acceptable excuse for dodging invitations at least one night a week, and it was there he had met Lynne. She looked like an angel to him with her halo of dark blonde curls and wide smile. They spent every free moment together and he was happy finally to have someone. It lasted almost a year. Then his angel used her wings.

The same free spirit nature that had attracted him to her in the beginning proved to be their relationship's downfall. It had been exactly one week since Lynne had shown him the door. She claimed he was stifling her and that she needed to get herself back. He blamed their breakup on her getting involved in macho adventure stuff. Weren't things fine the way they were? Why did she have to screw things up? She tried to explain her need for independence and space. When he told her she was crazy and should get counseling, she replied that she had been doing just that.

"Well, what does your counselor say?" he asked.

"She completely supports my decision."

"She? Well that explains it," Tim said, gritting his teeth and turning away.

The pain was as much physical as emotional when she told

him it was over. He had surprised himself with the anger in his voice when she had suggested they remain friends. "Friends? You might as well tell me to drop dead."

Over pitchers of beer with a couple of his more disreputable acquaintances, he'd worked himself into a rage. He'd known about the upcoming trip to Dragons Den; they'd argued about it. With BJ and Jake urging him on, he masterminded a plan to go see for himself what it was that she'd chosen over him. That BJ claimed to know the cave and was willing to act as a guide seemed perfect to Tim at the time.

Now, he stared down at the pure white knob of calcite in his hands and then carefully set it on a ledge, out of the way. He wondered, for the moment, what he was doing in this dark, alien place with these two apes who seemed bent on destroying the fragile cave world around them.

Still, he was glad he wasn't alone. Only the day before, Tim had read a news brief over the air about five teenagers who had been rescued from Trout Rocks Cave in West Virginia. They had gotten lost but were found by one of the Search & Rescue Teams—cold, scared, and hungry, but unharmed. He suppressed a shudder, but was thankful the story had prompted him to wear his long-johns and flannel shirt underneath a windbreaker, and to throw in an extra set of batteries and some candy bars. He looked at BJ and Jake in their shorts and tee-shirts and shook his head.

He had expected to feel claustrophobic. To his surprise, however, once inside, he felt small and overwhelmed by the size of the first room. He aimed his flashlight in all directions. He wanted to yell at BJ and Jake to shut up so he could take it all in without their noisy stomping around. He winced as Jake crushed a can and tossed it into a rim pool. He could smell the beer in the air. When they weren't looking, he picked up the can and stuffed it in his knapsack.

Tim was drawn in by the silent sculptures of Dragons Den. He empathized with the beautiful formations that had been broken and were now lying in pieces on the ground. He had the urge to lie down next to them, curl up, and let the cave cover him up, layer by layer. Turn him to stone.

Tim surreptitiously packed up the Destructive Duo's trash and distracted them away from some of the prettier formations with questions about possible pits and tunnels. A couple of times they'd left him behind. He searched wildly and held back panic as he called out for them. Something told him if he let them see how freaked he was left alone like that, they'd turn it into a devilish game of hide and seek. So he scrambled madly to keep up, trying to memorize the route.

Although BJ and Jake talked big about narrow passages and gaping pits, Tim noticed they avoided going into either. They were more interested in finding things to climb. Then they came to the pit with the colorful ropes and webbing secured at the top.

"Check this out," said BJ, fingering the pink webbing that encircled a large boulder. "Someone's down there. Shh, listen! I can hear voices in the pit. Man, it must be really deep, I can't see a damn thing. Here, shine your lights in the hole. C'mon Tim."

The three leaned over the edge and the lights of their flashlights vanished into the depths.

"Wow!" BJ said. "I can hear 'em. It's women! It's all chicks, man. I don't believe it."

"Naw, there must be guys too," Jake said. "Girls wouldn't know how to set all this stuff up."

"Just listen," BJ said. "Do you hear any guys? I tell you, it's all chicks. Hey, Tim, I think we just found your girlfriend."

Tim couldn't believe Lynne would have the guts to go down into that place. But she had. His hurt and jealousy were making him ill. She wanted adventure? She was about to get it. And it served her right. But he tried. "Come on you guys, just leave them alone."

"Oh, don't be such a wuss, man. You've been Mr. Clean all day long. Lighten up. Have some fun, dude. We're not gonna hurt no body. In fact, I have the perfect plan," BJ said, throwing an arm over Jake's shoulder.

"What?" Jake teetered unsteadily near the edge of the pit.

"We'll pull up their ropes, real quiet, and go away for a little while. We won't undo anything, we'll just pull 'em up and do a little more exploring. Then when we come back we'll say, 'Oh my God, did someone pull up your ropes?' and we'll lower 'em down and they'll be eternally grateful! They'll never know it was us that pulled the ropes up, people mess around in this cave all the time. It'll teach Tim's little lady a lesson, and maybe snag us a babe as well. I can't wait to meet some chicks that aren't afraid of a little adventure, can you?" The color rose in BJ's face and a shiver of excitement seemed to generate even more goosebumps on his exposed flesh. "I can't hear 'em now so they must be far enough away that they won't see the ropes being pulled up. C'mon." Without waiting for the other two, BJ began pulling up one of the ropes, motioning to Jake to haul up the other.

"You shouldn't be doing this, man," Tim's voice cracked.

"Hey, we're gonna put 'em back. We're not hurtin' no body. Just shut up and you'll see. After a couple of hours in that pit, your woman will never want to go off on her own again. I can hear her now when you pull her out of there." He moaned in a high falsetto, "Oh, Timmy, my hero."

Jake laughed until he remembered he was supposed to be doing the job quietly.

"Look, they're going to get pretty scared when they come back and find their ropes gone," Tim said. "Maybe you should put them back."

"We will, we will. We won't go far and I'm sure we'll be able to hear 'em holler for help. That's when we'll come to the rescue. I hope she has a red headed friend down there."

Tim walked away uneasily. He did want to be Lynne's hero, but this was perhaps the wrong way to go about it. "She deserves the scare," he tried to convince himself. "She's just asking for trouble by doing this stuff. Once she gets a feel for what it would be like to be alone in a scary situation, she won't go running off looking for adventure." He leaned against the cold cave wall, watching silently as BJ and Jake finished pulling the ropes up into a tangled pile.

"OK," BJ said, dusting his hands off on his shorts, "Let's mess around for a while to give 'em a chance to find out their ropes are gone. Man, I can't wait to hear 'em start screamin.'" He paused, looking up at a tempting passageway high in the wall behind the pit. "Looks like a good climb." Despite his semi-inebriated state, he moved like a lizard, flitting wildly up the rocks. "Easy climb," he called down to Jake and Tim. "Check out this overhang." A huge flat boulder protruded over him, and he could see an opening above and beyond it. "Come on, you guys, let's check out this high lead."

Jake followed him up, glancing at Tim as if daring him to object. Tim shifted uncomfortably as he calculated the height of the climb. It was a good thirty feet and he was not a rock jock like the other two. But there seemed to be enough ledges to hold on to, and it would keep his mind off the situation below.

He put his hands on the first rock and blew out a breath in shock as it shifted slightly with his weight. His eyes wildly sought BJ and Jake who were making their way up the unstable wall; he could no longer see anything of BJ other than his boots working their way up higher. The boots stopped and Jake hollered out, "What's wrong?"

Tim froze, listening. Why did BJ stop? BJ's retort was cut off in mid-sentence and the question hung suspended. What was that? A whimper? He couldn't imagine that kind of noise coming from BJ. And what was that grating, shifting sound? Stone scraping against stone with a heavy urgency. Tightening every muscle in his body, he clung by his shaking fingertips, bracing himself for something his body seemed to know but his mind could not accept. He felt the shock before he heard it, the rocks giving way beneath the climbers above. BJ's unbelieving scream and the inhuman sound of Jake's cry behind the rumbling mad collapse of stone. The world was sliding, crumbling, obliterating them. He closed his eyes, petrified, as he was shoved downward. It was all in slow motion but going so fast he couldn't think.

When Tim landed, sitting, at the bottom of it all, he thought for a second he had miraculously survived unscathed. But the cave wasn't through with him yet. Its final sad shudder sent one last chunk scraping and sliding down the rubble.

He flung himself onto his hands and knees to crawl out of the boulder's path. A scream strangled from his throat as it landed squarely on his leg. The scent of fear swirled around him. A weak beam from his small flashlight, dropped in the fall, disappeared into the dust-filled air. He reached over and turned it off, plunging himself into oblivious darkness. Before he passed out he realized that he was pinned near a mountain of rocks covering the hole.

3

Putting on Armor

Her first thought was of thunder.

"Oh my God, what was that?" Gabby said, grabbing Danielle by the arm.

Six pairs of anxious eyes sought Danielle's.

"I don't know," Danielle said. "Nicole, do you think we'd better go back and check the drop?"

"Definitely. I didn't like the sound of that."

"OK, let's all just stay calm until we see what it was," Danielle said, retracing her steps back to their ropes. Her voice was steady but her heart was pounding. They had gone exploring down the main passage of the lower level toward the waterfall when the roar and vibrations reached them. She forced herself to walk at a controlled pace, silently chanting the Prayer for Protection and steeling herself for whatever lay ahead.

"Please let the ropes be there, please let the ropes be there," she whispered. Kate grabbed her gloved hand and looked up at her mother for reassurance. Danielle wished she could be more certain that their alarm was for naught. She looked down at Kate's trusting face and squeezed her hand.

"What's wrong? What was that awful noise?" Gabby said, breaking out of the single file line and catching up to Danielle.

"It's probably just some breakdown somewhere in the cave.

33

Let's hope it wasn't near our ropes. Don't panic, get back in line; we'll know soon enough." Danielle quickened her pace. She could hear Lynne and Melissa whispering urgently. She knew she had to keep everyone moving and find out.

"Please let the ropes be there . . ." Danielle prayed.

Boulders and smaller rocks lay scattered beneath the drop. The ropes were gone.

Danielle sank to her knees. Where in the world were the ropes? She tilted her head back to look for the hole they had come through. With all their lights pointed up, they could see that it was plugged with boulders.

For a long desperate moment, no one moved. They held their breath, unable to swallow or speak.

Danielle felt like throwing up. She had a metallic, hollow taste in her mouth, like she'd been chewing on nails. She clasped Kate tightly to her side, knowing that when reality sank in, it could devastate the group. Her mind worked frantically, knowing she would have to take control before anyone dissolved into hysteria. If she threw herself into that task, maybe, just maybe, her own fear wouldn't overwhelm her.

"I want to go home," Lynne said in a quavering voice. "Get us out of here." Her words echoed against the dark walls as she stumbled to where rocks lay in a jumbled heap beneath the drop.

"Mom? Mommy? What are you gonna do?" Kate's face paled as she realized that these adults were scared.

"Hang on. Hang on," Danielle said, as much to herself as to the rest. Melissa was hugging Lynne in an effort to calm her. Nicole was sitting Gabby down since she looked ready to pass out. Danielle concentrated on her breathing, forcing the air in and out of her lungs until she could think clearly again. Think. Stay calm. Hold on. Sort out your thoughts and get a plan.

"Everyone come here," she said. "Sit close together and listen up."

"But Danielle, we're trapped, aren't we? I knew I shouldn't have come on this trip. We're never gonna get out of here." Gabby yanked her helmet off and dropped it with a clatter on the floor.

"Stop shouting," Danielle said. "No one can hear you and you'll just wear yourself out. Gabby, put that helmet back on."

"Please. Sit down and we'll figure something out."

"I've got to get out of here." Lynne began clambering over the rocks and flailed wildly at the cave walls.

Melissa quickly walked over and put a hand on Lynne's shoulder. "This is not our fault; something's happened that we had no control over."

"Don't touch me. I'm getting out of here." Lynne twisted away from Melissa, and spun around crazily, her light glancing off the terrified faces of the women around her. "What about my kids?"

"The quicker we can help each other get out of here, the quicker you'll get home to your children," Nicole said. "Come on, you're only making yourself more upset. Help us figure out a plan." She held out her hand.

Lynne wrapped her arms around herself and flopped down near the group, her bottom lip trembling. Sydney reached over and patted her muddy knee. Lynne began rocking, staring at the ground.

"OK," Danielle chose her words slowly and carefully. "The ropes are gone. And from what I can see, something must have happened up above because the hole seems to be covered up. Someone had to have pulled the ropes up; they're not down here."

"Who would do something like that?" Melissa was shaking her head and looking from face to face.

"I don't know. And it doesn't matter now. The point is, we can't go back up the way we came." Danielle forced herself to breathe slowly.

"So how are you going to get us out of here?" Gabby asked, sinking to the ground and huddling close to Lynne.

"Well, we do have a call-back with Max for 5:00 tomorrow afternoon," Danielle said slowly.

"You mean we have to wait down here until then?" Gabby jumped up and Lynne joined her in alarm. "But most of our stuff is back in the Dragon's Dining Room. How will we survive until then?"

"We have supplies in our packs, remember? The main thing is to keep our wits and work together. Freaking out isn't going to help anyone, it will only use up energy we need to get through this." Danielle spoke with as much conviction as she could muster. She needed to hear her own advice as much as the others did. She closed her eyes for a second and tried to calm her pounding heart by sheer mental will.

"What about air? Is there enough air down here? Oh my God, we're going to suffocate," Gabby rasped, her hands encircling her throat.

"No, no, now listen. Remember that there's a waterfall down on this level. We were almost to it when this all happened. That waterfall drops from the upper level and air gets through. We have plenty of air; the drop isn't the only place where the lower level is connected."

"Is there another way out?" Sydney asked hopefully. "Where does the waterfall go?"

At that moment, Lynne gave a low moan and crumpled to the muddy floor, overcome with fright and shock. Nicole immediately took a hypothermia blanket from her pack and wrapped it around Lynne's prone body to keep her warm. Then she grabbed Kate's pack and put it under Lynne's feet to get the blood back to her head, and instructed Melissa to get out some water and a powerbar.

"You're OK," Nicole said, smoothing a few strands out of Lynne's face. "This is pretty overwhelming, isn't it? We have to try not to panic."

"I think we'd better get everyone warmed up and fed," Sydney said. "We can't think straight if we're cold and hungry on top of being scared."

"You're right, Sydney," Danielle said. "Let's move to that flat spot over there and wrap up in our hypothermia blankets. We'll pool everything from our packs and see what we've got to work with. Nicole, how's Lynne doing now? If she's not warm enough I've got some of those little heat packs you can stick in there with her."

"I'll live," Lynne said. "Just give me a few minutes. I'm sorry I flipped out on ya'll like that. This is really scary."

"I know. I'm sorry about all this. Nicole, why don't you help Lynne move over here once she catches her breath a little more." Danielle moved some rocks aside.

"Sure thing," Nicole said. "And ya'll are gonna love this; remember up in the Dining Room when you razzed me about my little stove? Well, guess what I have in my pack?"

"Good thinking, Nicole," Danielle said. "Let's get a hot drink into everyone and we'll start figuring out a game plan." She began taking stock of what was in the packs. She thought a moment of Max, exactly where he was and what he was doing this very moment, but he couldn't help her here now. She was glad the group had begun to focus on survival, but shivered at the thought that even though they had a 5:00 p.m. call back, that didn't mean they would be rescued by then. When they didn't call in, Max would initiate the rescue procedures, but it would take a few hours to organize and search the cave. Once they saw whatever the problem was at the drop, they would either have to clear the rocks from the hole or try to find another way to reach them. But to tell the group that now would be like putting gasoline on a fire. Better to focus on staying alive for the moment.

Danielle was already a survivor. She remembered the day her doctor had told her the lump in her right breast was malignant. A lump in her breast, like the lump of rock up above blocking passage to life and the future. She had to make decisions then, too. After analyzing the pro's and con's with surgeons and oncologists, friends and family, she'd gone the least traumatic route, a lumpectomy, a lymphectomy, and radiation to her breast. As she lay on the radiation table at lunch time every weekday for those eight weeks, she visualized first a courageous knight in armor using the radiation beam as his lance to slay the cancer-dragon. Then finally she decided she would be her own knight and overcome that dragon herself. The doctor's, "All fifteen lymph nodes are clean," assured her she'd made the right decision. Now the cancer was three years behind her and she considered herself whole and well. She tucked that thought under her belt, as if it were a mighty sword. She had only to believe in herself, in her daughter and the women with her, and in Max and the others who would help from the outside. She was not facing this dragon alone.

4

Peripheral Vision

"Just relax and trust me," Max called up to the teenager who was clinging to the rock with a Vulcan Death Grip at the top of the cliff. "I've got you on belay. You climbed great. Now, just let go like you did before, I've got you."

Max took up what little slack was left in the rope and pulled the tail end of the rope down and back within the ATC on his harness to brake the boy's descent. The ATC was appropriately named the Air Traffic Controller, a device used to belay climbers. Max's bearded face was a study of concentration. A self-proclaimed adrenaline junkie, he was in his element teaching others. It was thrilling when he rappelled 680 feet off the New River Gorge Bridge on Bridge Day, or climbed a new route up the front of Tunstalls Tooth, but his greatest satisfaction came from seeing the lightbulb go on over a student's head when he applied one of the techniques Max had taught him, or from hearing the pride in a student's voice when she climbed a route she thought she'd never make. Danielle called him a Renaissance man. Besides climbing and caving, he'd earned a black belt in Shaolin-Su Kempo. Both of them played guitar and sang in local coffeehouses, enjoying the rush that came through connecting with an audience.

"Falling!" the young man called, no longer able to hold on. He swung away from the rocky wall. Max smiled as he noted the boy's audible sigh of relief as he hung in his harness from the rope. Max lowered him gently to the ground. Although the boy was blind, like the other three high school students at this special class, he beamed in Max's direction, obviously proud of himself. "That was great," he said. "It gets better every time. Thanks."

Max gave the boy a pat on the back and readied the next student for her climb. The idea for working with blind kids had actually come about over a Volcano he and Danielle had drunk at one of the local Chinese restaurants. It was back when Max had first started teaching Danielle how to climb and they'd had a satisfying day on the rocks at Fools Face. As she'd tentatively made her way up the rock, he had called up moves and directions to her. "Use that finger pocket to your right. Put your left foot on that flake by your knee." Every inch of the way. Danielle, feeling a little silly from the drink (complete with fire burning in the center of the gaudy ceramic glass), said Max must know the beginner route so well that he could probably do it blindfolded. Max liked the idea and accepted her challenge on their next trip. It had added a whole new dimension to what Max called the "pucker factor" of the climb, and had honed his other senses to an ever finer degree. Halfway up his sightless climb, the thought occurred to him that if climbing was such a confidence builder, why not offer it to the blind? Since then he'd added blindfolded climbs to his repertoire to keep his skills sharp and his empathy intact.

Although he was enjoying being out on the rocks and working with the students, his attention kept wandering miles away to Dragons Den. It wasn't that he was worried about Danielle's abilities; he knew she was careful—overly cautious, if anything. And Nicole knew her stuff too. But always something could go wrong.

When the climbing class was over, Max drove home, backing his truck up the driveway to the building he'd designed and constructed himself. Upstairs was Danielle's art studio, their music equipment, and office; downstairs was all the caving, camping, and climbing gear, as well as a workshop. Originally he'd only planned to build a small one-room storage shed, but by the time he'd finished it was two-stories tall with a bi-level deck.

He started putting away the day's climbing gear, then paused with a rope bag in hand. If there was a rescue, he might as well be ready to roll. He could play Murphy's Law and jinx the need for a rescue by being prepared for one. There'd be no harm in having everything in the truck. He packed every bit of equipment he could possibly need—ropes, pulleys, rigging plates, edge pro, cave pack, first aid kit, blankets, map of Dragons Den, military field telephones, and a special flexible stretcher called a sked used for carrying someone through tight cave passages. Sweat beaded his brow as he stuffed in the last piece of equipment. He sat down wearily on the tailgate. He hoped he wouldn't need to use the stuff.

"I'll go out to the land for a while. That always makes me feel better. Hike around a bit and chill out." Max stopped at the Orange Market to get a cup of ice water and some fresh fruit to eat on the way. He distracted himself by going over their house plans in his head. Well, it was her first trip as leader, after all.

Max had fallen in love with Catawba Valley long before he met Danielle. She, too, had found it on her own and vowed to live there. With this dream in common, it was only natural that they spent their free weekends driving through its lush woodlands, pastures, and fields of silver queen corn looking for tempting FOR SALE signs. "We need a buffer" they agreed, "a few acres where we can build a house and keep the wildness surrounding us; an oasis; a retreat from the city where we can flourish."

When they first heard of Murder Hole, the name had made Danielle shudder. Years of teaching herself to think positive were challenged by such a formidable appellation. Although they were familiar with many of the local caves, they had the mistaken impression that Murder Hole was on the steep side of the mountain and not in a site suitable for building. But one summer day, a real estate agent suggested they ride out and look at the property. When told it was in the heart of the valley they loved, they readily agreed to go see it.

They would never forget that day. They drank in the fresh air as they drove past family farms and faded barns. Black and white cows milled at a roadside gate, waiting to cross the narrow country road. A sparkling creek flowed under a one-lane bridge, and wound on through fertile pasture land. A rusted out pick-up truck and ancient gas pump kept company in front of an abandoned country store, overgrown with wild grapevines. Cedars and tulip trees, blackberry bushes and orange wood lilies added color and texture to the landscape's tapestry. They smiled at the iridescent flash of a blue bird as they swerved around a box turtle crossing the road. This land seemed to reach out to them and say, "Welcome home."

They turned off the road onto a rough, rocky dirt road that climbed Gravely Ridge, whose arched back rises like a humpback whale in the undulating topography of Catawba Valley. They parked the truck and continued on foot, breathing heavily more with expectation than exertion. This land was the place they'd both seen in their dreams. Their search was over. But there was more.

Danielle had seen it first, and the look on Max's face was priceless as he came round the bend and stopped, catching his breath before the vast hole in the ground. So this was Murder Hole! A grotto where the roof of the cave had collapsed ages ago, leaving a gaping void 130 feet deep, 100 feet across and 70 feet wide. You could fit an eight story building into it. Dogwoods, columbine, foxglove, and mountain laurel grew around it, and jack-in-the-pulpits and lacy ferns lined the walls of the lower levels. If you looked closely, you could see evidence of formations along some of the walls, now eroded by the elements and lush vegetation. Standing at the brink, you could look up at the horizon and see McAfees Knob, and then look down and see the impressive depths of the Daylight Cave portion of Murder Hole.

They considered it a miracle that their offer on the thirty-four acres was accepted and they became owners—or stewards as they liked to say—of this adventurers' wonderland. Danielle even carried a picture in her wallet of the view looking up out of the Daylight Cave. They loved to look up at the blue sky, framed by the towering walls of the cave, and watch the clouds go by. "If you pretend the clouds aren't moving," Danielle would say, "it makes it seem like the cave is a giant ship and we're the ones in motion." The rest of their dream was awaiting completion. They planned to build their home on the ridge, just past Murder Hole.

He parked and got out. The bright red head of a woodpecker flashed through the leaves at him, rapping out a drum solo to his footsteps up the road. He stripped off his sweaty T-shirt and tucked it under his belt next to his knife. He searched the woods for other familiar wildlife, while his heart searched for peace to soothe the unnamed fear that wouldn't leave him alone.

This was the first time he had been in a search mode since Danielle came into his life. As a child he had searched for his father. As a teenager he had searched for an identity, and then for reasons for the military's secret war that he was not allowed to talk about. As a betrayed husband by his first wife, he had searched for a way to spend time with a daughter who had been taken from him; first by her mother, then by a fatal car accident. As a police officer he had searched for justice and control over a world that often made no sense. And as a man he had searched for a woman who was not afraid of his destiny, or her own.

He had slept with a gun next to his bed until Danielle had taken up permanent residence there.

He sat down on the wooden retaining wall he'd built to keep the dirt road from washing down the talus slope, a nearly vertical path that dropped more than a hundred feet into the Daylight Cave of Murder Hole. He grabbed a sassafras sapling broken by a recent summer storm and idly whittled the bark off of it with his knife, enjoying the fragrant smell of wet wood. Every time the image of Danielle and the group in the cave appeared in his brain, he mentally refocused on something else in an attempt to keep from worrying. He thought about the house they would build, wishing it was there already so he could walk into the kitchen, fix himself a cup of coffee, and sit on the back deck, contemplating McAfees Knob and all the hikers who must be up there on the Appalachian Trail. But around and around his mind went, coming back every time to Dragons Den. He sighed. Danielle was fine. Kate too. Stop worrying.

Out of the corner of his eye he saw a rock undulate. No. Not the rock. Something underneath it in some dead leaves. His nostrils flared at the faint scent of cucumbers. Copperhead! Over two feet of camouflaged, deadly beauty. Max hated poisonous snakes. He didn't care if it wasn't environmentally correct. If he knew where to get King Snakes, he'd scatter a few around to do the job. This was a big copperhead that apparently lived within striking distance of the wall where they often sat at dusk to watch the bats do their twilight dance. He rose slowly. The snake watched him, flickering its tongue. Max moved stealthily around the rocks until he was out of the snake's line of sight. With his left hand he aimed the point of the carved sapling at the snake's hideout, coiling his own muscles for the split second the snake would strike. Sssst! As the snake lunged, Max's boot clamped down on its neck, his knife flashing sunlight as he severed the snake's head. The body writhed and whiplashed. Max waited, heart pounding, then picked up the golden patterned body by the tail and flung it onto a large flat rock. He skinned the snake, marveling at the complexity of the colors and designs of its hide.

When he finally looked up, the first few bats were winging their way out of the cave for their evening meal. Max watched them for a while, then got into his truck and drove home.

5

Trial by Stone

"BJ? Where are you, BJ?" Jake cried out in the darkness, flicking on his cigarette lighter and rising unsteadily to his feet atop the precarious rock pile. In the lighter's dim flame he saw the butt of a flashlight sticking out of the rubble. He groped his way to it, then turned it on. The light caught BJ's face, his tangle of dusty red hair contrasting sharply with the bluish white pallor of his skin.

"Throw me your light, I think my arm's busted." BJ twisted himself out of the rock-pile, sending a few more stones skittering down the heap.

"Look out man, you're making it worse." Jake picked his way gingerly around the worst of the breakdown, then froze when he saw Tim's motionless form at the foot of the pile. "This is the only flashlight we got, I'm not gonna throw it. Look, you're bleeding." Jake reached out to BJ's arm only to be shoved brusquely aside.

"I know. It hurts like hell. Let's get out of here."

"But, aren't we gonna check on Tim first? What if he's still alive? We have to see if he's . . ."

"You do it. Hurry up. We have to get out of here, fast." BJ pulled his T-shirt over his head and wound it around his injured arm. They worked their way down the rocks, to where Tim lay.

Jake dropped to his knees, "Tim? Tim? Can you hear me?" As

49

if expecting Tim to jump up and grab him at any moment, Jake warily held his hand near Tim's open mouth. "I can feel his breath. He's not dead. We have to get that rock off of him and . . ."

"We'll go for help. We can't get him out of here by ourselves. Look, man, my arm's busted and your head's bleeding."

"It is? Oh shit," Jake said, sitting down shakily. "I can't believe we're not all dead." They both jumped as Tim moaned faintly.

"We'll be lucky to get our own asses out of here alive. We'll call for help as soon as we get out." BJ faltered, averting his eyes from Jake's dismayed face. "Please?"

Jake opened his mouth to protest, then shut it, realizing that BJ had said 'Please.' It was unnerving. "Are you sure he'll be okay?" Jake said. "It's so cold in here."

"The quicker we get him help, the better off he'll be. Let's go. And wrap something around your head before you bleed to death."

"BJ," Jake stopped dead in his tracks, imagining anguished faceless women suddenly screaming at him from somewhere below his feet. "What about the . . . the others?"

BJ looked away, working his jaw as if the words themselves were bits of stone left in his mouth by the breakdown. "I told you, we'll call for help once we're out." BJ nudged Jake, "Now, move!"

Tim was being devoured. Stone jaws ground down on his leg. An unforgiving monster dragging him slowly downward into darkness. His nerve endings exploded messages to his brain. "God it hurts. Let me go," Tim begged. Pain shot through him and radiated into his hip, turning lights on in his stunned mind, wrenching him into the dizzy red world of agony.

He remembered the collapse. The final rock falling on him before he could crawl out of the way.

He fumbled frantically for his flashlight, feeling around blindly over dirt and rock . . . there. He grasped the cold metal handle and felt for the button.

How could everything look so still and calm and quiet? Deathly quiet. No sign of BJ or Jake; they must have been buried beneath the rock-slide. A few motes of cave dust hung suspended in the flashlight's beam.

He twisted around painfully to see how big the rock on his leg

was, but his eyes widened in alarm as he looked beyond the boulder to the rock pile covering the pit. Lynne! And he was going to be her hero. He moaned and spit into the dirt.

The boulder on his leg didn't look that big. It seemed as though he should be able to push it off. But it wouldn't budge, and he realized he was using up valuable energy. He began the tedious process of scooping out the dry, crumbly dirt from around his leg. He stopped every few minutes to push the pain down and catch his breath. The flashlight grew dimmer and he turned it off, much as he hated the darkness. He felt feral, reduced to survival instincts. He remembered years ago jumping off a cliff into a quarry lake and wondering if he'd never make it back up to the surface. "Gotta get out of here," he groaned and continued clawing away at the dirt.

During one of his rests, he turned the feeble light back on to look for his pack. There it was, just a few feet away, but beyond his reach. The exertion of his digging chased his chills away for a while, but he knew he had to get free and reach his pack to have any chance at all.

As he scraped more dirt from under the rock, he tried to blot out thoughts of BJ and Jake. His anger had nowhere left to turn but inward; they had already been punished. Their punishment was greater, but maybe more merciful, he thought. Another wave of pain made him scream in a voice he didn't recognize.

The irony bore down on him. Lynne had said he was stifling her. How unbearably true; he'd brought the cave down on top of her. Buried her alive.

"Got to get out, get help. If it's the last thing I do. Have to get Lynne out." He dug some more. Eventually he felt the rock's hold loosen and he pulled forward, bit by bit, dragging his poor leg out from under the boulder. The skin was not broken on his leg. There was no blood, only mind-numbing pain throbbing up from broken bones and huge contusions. He bit down on his lip, drawing blood as he forced himself to feel his battered leg for damage. It was at an odd angle and some of the bones seemed to be rearranged beneath the skin. He dragged himself over to his pack, knowing he needed to eat to hold onto his fading consciousness.

The faces of Lynne's three children appeared in his mind. Laughing and tussling and bickering in typical sibling rivalry.

Luminous brown eyes both wary and craving attention. "Are you going to be our new daddy?" He couldn't remember why he was so scared of them. Perhaps because they seemed to look right through him. What did he have to offer them? Lynne was an endless source of love for them. How could she have enough to love him too? But she thought nothing of opening herself to him and giving and giving. But what if he had nothing to give back? Well, now he had plenty to give. He'd take on loving them all if he could only get out to bring back help.

He opened his pack and took out a candy bar. His hands were shaking, so he tore open the wrapper with his teeth. Fighting the pain in his leg, he chewed the chocolate slowly, not tasting it.

One night, just before they split up, they were having one of their final arguments in Lynne's country kitchen, surrounded by her black and white cow knickknacks and blue crockware. Their battle screeched to a halt at the appearance of her three-year old, cheeks shiny with tears, and a stuffed animal (hugged and squeezed beyond recognition) clutched tightly in her arms. "Mommy, I'm scared."

Lynne knelt by her little daughter and hugged her close, "What's wrong, punkin', did you have a bad dream?"

"Uh huh, a monster was going to get me. He's in my room."

Tim waved his hand and bellowed, "Just put her back in bed. That's stupid, there's no monsters in there."

Lynne whirled to face him, "See what I mean? You don't care about how other people feel. Of course there are no monsters, but everyone has fears and bad dreams sometimes. She needs someone to hug her and reassure her; not someone to tell her she's stupid." Gathering up her sniffling daughter she said, "Just leave us alone. We can take care of ourselves."

As Lynne turned to leave the room, Tim reached out and grabbed her roughly by the arm, spinning her around to face him.

"You'd better think about this before you walk out on me. I could have anyone I want, you know."

"Fine," she said. "Go have anyone you want. But you're not having me."

That did it. Before he realized it he'd . . . No point in dragging that all up now. What he'd done now was far worse.

"God, I do need you," Tim whispered into the dirt at his chin.

The candy bar gave him the strength to crawl down the passage away from the breakdown site. Thanks to the extra set of batteries he'd thrown in at the last minute, his light was strong again. But now it shone on a major obstacle, a ledge some four feet high. He hadn't given it a second thought on the way in, but now it appeared insurmountable. It was either pull himself up, or crawl back and search for a different passage.

But now his brain reeled with the effort of suppressing his pain and trying to remember the way out. He couldn't get his bearings. Was he headed the right way? Maybe not; maybe he should take the small passage a few yards back. He didn't know. He turned around and starting crawling the other way.

His voice echoed off the stone walls, "This is Tim Stephenson, your WKAV-fm Country Music Cowboy, broadcasting live from the depths of hell. Yes, my faithful listeners, your beloved DJ has ridden off into the land of no sunset. Today's weather is cold and dark, with a hundred percent chance of rock showers." His voice droned on, becoming incoherent as his body cooled in hypothermia.

6

One Small Light

"Feel a little better now?" Danielle asked, looking around at her comrades cocooned in silver space blankets like astronauts preparing for a galactic journey. They huddled together, sitting on their knee pads to keep the cold floor from sucking the heat from their bodies.

Kate played with a cylume stick, which they were using for light in the interest of saving batteries, her dark, expressive eyebrows scrunched into a frown. "What time is it, mom?"

"It's about 7:00."

"Morning or night?" The eerie chartreuse of the fluorescent light-stick lit up Kate's face as she studied its glow.

"Yeah," Lynne sighed. "I've lost all perspective of time down here. No sun, no moon, I'm going nuts."

"It's Saturday night. And that's a good point, Lynne. We need to keep track of that. Especially for when our call-back is."

"I've got a pen and some paper in my pack," Melissa said. "I never know when I'm going to get inspired to write a poem or something. I can keep a journal for us. Who knows, after we get out of here maybe we can collaborate on a cave ballad."

"If we ever get out of here," mumbled Lynne. "How can you think about writing a song? Unless you want to sing the blues."

"Let's inventory our supplies so we can ration our food and batteries" Nicole said. She and Danielle exchanged glances as the pile grew, glad they had made each person bring a day's worth. She tried not to think about the supplies and sleeping bags back in the Dragon's Dining Room.

"Shoot, it looks like we have enough to get us through to our call-back time. That's less than 24 hours away, right?" Gabby looked expectantly at Danielle and Nicole. "Right?"

Danielle swallowed and tried to choose her words carefully. She took off her helmet and the bandanna she wore over her long braided hair. She removed her gloves and ran her fingers through her matted bangs. "You're right, Gabby. Our call-back time is 5:00 p.m. But the thing is, that's just when Max will start the rescue when he doesn't hear from us. It's going to take him some time to contact the other cavers, get them organized, search the cave, and figure out what happened." She braced herself for the reactions of her team-mates as the grim reality sank in.

Lynne rose, eyes wide and voice shaking, "How much time?"

"I'm sure they'll move as fast as they can." Danielle hoped her voice sounded confident and optimistic, grateful the others couldn't hear her heart pounding.

Everyone sank into gloomy silence, contemplating the implications of what was left unsaid. Kate waved the light stick around in front of her as if trying to paint the darkness with its light. Then she paused it mid-air, "But, Mom, how are they going to get us out? The hole's all covered up."

Danielle winced. The policy in the Stewart family was always to tell the truth.

Sydney asked quickly, "Is there another way out of here? Besides the way we came in?"

Everyone spoke at once, begging for answers.

"Sssh," Danielle said. "I can't think when you're all talking at once. The way I see it, there are only two options."

"The waterfall?"

Sydney had been studying the cave and comparing it to other caves she'd been in. She remembered waiting her turn to ascend the rope out of Sinks of the Run Cave in West Virginia; the spray of the waterfall near the drop had prompted her to wrap up in her hypothermia blanket while the caver ahead of her climbed up with prussik knots.

"The waterfall is one possibility," Danielle said. "But unfortunately the opening at the top isn't big enough for a person to fit through."

"I could fit through," Kate said.

"Honey, the top of the waterfall is a hundred feet above us. How would you get up to it? We don't have any ropes, remember? Even if we had ropes, we'd have to be able to fly to get them up there. But, the rescue team might be able to open it up enough to get someone through if they had to."

"How would they widen it?" Gabby asked. "With hammers and chisels?"

"Well, it would probably take dynamite."

Lynne's eyes widened in alarm. "Dynamite! But wouldn't that make the cave collapse? What if it came down on us?"

Nicole turned on her helmet light and pulled the Dragons Den map out of her pack. "They'd check everything out very carefully before doing that. And they probably won't try to reach us through the drop if it's covered with unstable boulders."

Melissa asked, "What's the other way, Danielle? Is it the stream passage? Could we follow the stream out of the cave?"

"That's what I was thinking too." Sydney freed her pale hand from its muddy glove to finger the crystal necklace she always wore. The solitary light of Nicole's helmet caught its facets and arced into a tiny rainbow on Sydney's chin.

"Look," Danielle said, pointing over Nicole's shoulder at the map. "We're here, not far from the waterfall. I know we could make it that far. I've done it once before. But from there we'd have to climb down a cliff to follow the stream. Max and a few of the Grotto folks have pushed on through some breakdown and were stopped where the water sumps."

"Sumps? What's that?" Gabby looked ready to bolt, or keel over.

"It means the stream flows down through a tunnel and comes out on the other side," Sydney said.

"Right—a siphon," Danielle added slowly. "There's probably no air in it. We'd have to hold our breath and swim through."

Gabby blanched but Kate was quick to announce that she was an excellent swimmer. "How far?" Gabby asked. "How far would you have to swim?"

"I'm not sure. According to the map it looks to be about thirty feet. No one has ever gone all the way through. They did put some dye in the water from this end and had someone confirm that it showed up at the resurgence, and just estimated the distance of the siphon. No point in any of them risking a swim when they could just go back out the way they came in," Danielle said. "So we don't know exactly how long the passage is or if it's wide enough for someone to fit through all the way."

"I can't swim," Gabby said. "I think we ought to just wait and let them come rescue us." She'd almost rather die waiting to be rescued than submerge her body in anything but a hot tub.

Danielle was silent. She looked over their cache of supplies, calculating how long before they ran out. By Sunday night, most of the food would be gone. And the drinking water soon after that, although they could boil water from the stream as long as Nicole's little stove held out. Danielle berated herself for not bringing purification tablets, but then, she hadn't planned on being in Dragons Den more than one night. Most of the women were already using their back-up set of batteries, and they were leaving most of the lights off to conserve them. But moving through the breakdown and climbing down the cliff would require each person to burn her light to see enough to be safe. They couldn't just sit passively waiting for the rescuers to reach them; it could be days.

Danielle's mind clicked away. If they moved on toward the siphon, leaving trail markers, they could make the attempt while they were still strong. If the rescuers broke through from above in the meantime, they could follow the trail and catch up to them before they had to risk swimming the siphon. Moving on would be better than sitting around waiting, and the activity would keep the group warm and focused.

Her intuition kept telling her to go for it. She could visualize the sunlight waiting on the other side. The hazy blue-green mountains and cerulean sky, and Max.

They talked about whether to wait or press on. Gabby begged vehemently to stay and wait. Lynne agreed with her, but said she'd do whatever it took to get home to her kids. Nicole said she could manage the swim, but suggested they'd have to strip down and wrap their clothes in their spare plastic bags to keep them dry. Otherwise they could get hypothermic making their way out of the rest of the cave on the other side. Kate, who'd been bragging about her swimming abilities, was suddenly silenced by the thought of having to disrobe in front of the others. Once assured that she could leave on her body-suit, she felt a little better about the idea. Sydney warned everyone that the water would be cold, in the fifties.

"That's okay," Nicole said, "it's not like we're going to want to take our time swimming through."

"Just don't take my picture, Gabby," Kate said, folding her arms in a mock huff.

"Hey, speaking of pictures, why aren't you taking any?" Melissa said.

"Now? You've got to be kidding." Gabby shivered, still worried about the thought of having to get into the water. "Why? For our obituaries?"

"No, I'm serious," Melissa said. "Don't most artists do their finest work under pressure? And when we get out you can print them in National Geographic. Isn't that every photographer's dream? Come on. I know I'll sure want some of your pictures for my scrapbook."

Gabby finally relented. She pulled the camera from the side pocket of her pack and began looking at each person through the lens, the familiar work calming her. She loved catching a glimpse of peoples' souls through the lens of her camera, and she clicked off some good shots as the plan was discussed thoroughly (and sometimes heatedly).

Danielle sat on her kneepads for warmth, using her pack as a backrest. Now and then she pulled her long hair around to re-braid the hopeless tangle into some semblance of order. Gabby had been surprised to learn that Danielle was forty; her energy and stamina made her appear younger. She had confided in Gabby that she liked to think of herself as the initially timid heroine in the movie "Romancing the Stone," her hair caught up in a bun and horn-rimmed glasses, slowly evolving into an adventurous woman, her hair flowing loose and free, surviving any dangerous escapade she was thrown into. Gabby adjusted the settings on the camera to get a photo of Danielle explaining her plan, drawing pictures on the cave floor so everyone could visualize what they had to do. She waited, then was rewarded with a poignant shot of Danielle stroking a few wisps of gold-brown hair out of her daughter's eyes.

Kate's eyes were a lighter brown than her mother's, but she had the same dark, expressive eyebrows. Gabby liked Kate's strong sense of self and independence. She was tall for her age, and muscular despite her thin build. And to her mother's exasperation, she liked to let her hair do its own thing, Gabby got a shot of Kate with her hair hanging defiantly down over her eyes.

Lynne's blonde curls fell to her shoulders, and there was usually a broad smile on her face. She was a 90's super-woman; raising three boisterous children single-handed, working full-time at the Super Walmart, and going to college two nights a week. She had a computer at home and was hoping to own her own business someday, designing web sites and doing consultations for small businesses. Gabby snapped a shot of Lynne laughing when Nicole pulled a tampon out of their pile of supplies and informed the group that it could come in handy for a nosebleed.

Nicole managed a brave smile as Gabby focused on her chiseled cheekbones and wispy black hair. Nicole had told Gabby that her thin frame was the result of being a dedicated vegetarian, and that she had to be extra careful about becoming hypothermic since she didn't have much padding on her bones. Nicole tilted her head slightly and touched her strong, delicate fingers to her forehead in a mock salute.

Melissa was frowning with concentration as she scribbled furiously on some mud-stained paper. She was keeping a journal of what they were doing. Melissa admitted she was always getting inspired by something or someone; lately it had been Native Americans. She spent some time telling them about some of the Native American books she'd read. In the van on the way to the cave, Melissa had shown pictures from some buckskinner primitive rendezvous camps that she and her friends had participated in. Somehow Melissa looked natural in fringed moccasins, a leather beaded halter top, and breech clout. Melissa stopped writing and

looked up as if for a word from her muse, and at that moment Gabby snapped the shot.

At midnight, Danielle said they should all get some sleep in preparation for the next day's challenges. "We're going to have to really help each other tomorrow. So try to get some rest. I think we have a good plan."

For the last snapshot of the evening, Gabby balanced her camera on a rock and set the self-timer to capture her own face on film. What would finally emerge in the darkroom if she made it back home? Her gray-green eyes and tawny hair beside each high cheekbone? The underlying strength she was struggling to summon? Would you be able to see fear in the photo? Would it appear as an evil face lurking in the shadows and smiling over her shoulder? Or would you see the faint glow of the strength she felt radiating from the other women? As the last helmet light clicked off, Gabby tenderly tucked her camera safely in her pack.

The soft sounds of breathing were accompanied by an occasional drip and the leathery shuffle of batwings. No one was really sleeping; there was too much to think about. But they knew they had to rest. Danielle drew Kate closer to her in the darkness, whispering a soothing goodnight blessing.

"Mom, it's okay. Daddy's going to save us. I know he will."

"I'm sure he'll do his best, sweetie, but we're going to have to help save ourselves too. We can't just sit around waiting for him to do it for us."

"Wouldn't he be proud if we got out all by ourselves?" Kate said.

Danielle felt Kate sit up excitedly, and wished she could turn on a light to see her face. She reached out to touch Kate's cheek and could feel her daughter's one-dimple smile.

"He sure would. And we'd be proud of ourselves too. Wouldn't that be something to share at 'Show and Tell'? But now we need to get some sleep. We have a big day ahead of us, and I'm going to need your help."

Kate laid her head on Danielle's thigh and wrapped an arm protectively over it. "Mom, could you sing me a song? I think it would make me feel better." "Well, I don't want to disturb the others. They're trying to sleep too."

Melissa piped up, "It won't bother me. I'll even hum along with you." The other women urged them on. After a few moments, Danielle began, and Melissa wove in a clear, sweet harmony:

The crystal ballrooms of cave
Lie hidden in the dark
For centuries the magic waits
For that initial spark
Then one small light and you can see
The world unfold its mystery
No more loneliness or doubt
Your light has chased darkness out

The crystal ballrooms of my dreams
Were hidden in the dark
The magic in me had to wait
For that initial spark
Then one small light and I could see
The beauty deep inside of me
No more loneliness or doubt
My light had chased the darkness out

    It was there all along
    This wondrous world within
    Shining and strong
    Just waiting to begin

The crystal ballrooms of your dreams
May be hidden in the dark
The magic in you has to wait
For that initial spark
Then one small light and you can see
The beauty deep in you and me
No more loneliness or doubt
Your light can chase the darkness out

    It was there all along
    This wondrous world within

Shining and strong
Just waiting to begin
Waiting to begin . . .
Waiting to begin . . .

The final notes reverberated into the blanket of darkness, and the women wandered off into their separate dreams.

7

Challenges of Choice

Someone was crying. Danielle roused herself out of a fitful sleep and reached instinctively for Kate. No, she could feel Kate's ribs rising and falling, breathing quietly, regularly. Danielle gave herself a moment's luxury of envying the child's innocence and trust, then flicked on her light to see where the sobs were coming from. She was surprised to see it was Sydney. She gently moved Kate and crawled over.

"Sydney? Are you all right?"

Sydney raised red-rimmed eyes, "I thought I'd be better at this." She rummaged through her pack for something to wipe her runny nose. "Aren't you scared? You seem so strong and sure that we'll get out of here."

"You think I'm not scared? Oh Sydney, I . . . I'm . . ." The dam burst in Danielle, all the walls so carefully built around her suddenly cracked and let her own tears come pouring out. They reached out and held onto each other, letting the fear and fatigue wash over them.

Lynne groped her way over to the two sobbing women, "What's wrong?" She flicked her light on and aimed it toward their faces.

"Nothing. Oh, everything. And turn your light off, we need to save our batteries."

Lynne flipped the toggle switch on her helmet to turn her light off but was not to be put off. "Nothing wrong? Oh my, but why are you . . ." And she began to giggle uncontrollably, pointing at them.

Danielle grew indignant, "What? What's so funny?"

"You should see your faces. You look like the southbound end of a northbound baboon!" Lynne's hand shook as she laughed and pointed at the streaks left by tears on their muddy faces.

"Well you can't tell your face from your buddy mutt!" Sydney said, searching her handkerchief for a corner that she hadn't blown her nose into.

Still crying, Danielle retorted, "Hey, people pay fortunes for mud packs and beauty creams. You've heard of make-over's; well, this is a make-under. Anyway, you should see your hair."

"Yeah, helmet head," Sydney said, quickly reaching up self consciously to comb through her own tangled locks with her fingers.

The three dissolved into hysterical laughter, interspersed with coughs and hiccups. One by one, the rest woke and joined them, and they clung to each other, sometimes crying and wailing, but then laughing madly until they collapsed, spent, on the ground.

"Do you think we're losing our minds?" Lynne said. Her face felt swollen and her stomach hurt, but there was a glint of determination in her eyes.

Nicole hugged Melissa and Lynne who leaned on her from either side. "Actually, I think we've found them," she smiled. "I think we had to get it out of our systems or we would go crazy."

"Maybe we're laughing at ourselves because we know crying and getting mad won't do any good," Melissa said. "Kind of like when you lose something, or when someone you love dies."

"I wish you wouldn't talk about dying," Gabby said. "I'm not ready to die." She folded her arms across her chest and rubbed her hands up and down her arms to get warm.

"I didn't mean it like that. But that is what we're afraid of isn't it? We ought to talk about the death thing; face our fears. We each had, I mean have a great life ahead of us. None of us is ready to have it cut short, right?"

They glanced at each other, and shuffled their booted feet.

Kate stooped down and began piling up some rocks, "Let's make a time capsule, like the ones they bury or send out into space. Each person put something here in the pile for the rescuers to find, in case we don't make it."

"That's morbid," Lynne said, backing away a few steps.

"Well, it's not really thinking very positive," agreed Danielle, "but Kate's got a good idea, and maybe it will help us put our feelings in perspective." She paused. "If Melissa has some extra paper, we could each write a message to stick in the rock cairn. There are some things I'd like to say to Max, if . . ." her voice broke and she bent to find an extra zip-lock bag to put their messages in. She really did believe they would get out. And some last words seemed like a preventative measure. "You don't have to do it if you don't want to."

"Mom, what are you going to write? I was just going to leave my silver horse necklace. Daddy will know it came from me. And besides, in Heaven I'll have real horses to ride. Well, maybe not real, but I bet there'll be angel horses with wings, like Pegasus."

Danielle hugged Kate. Guilt rose as she held her daughter tightly. She shouldn't have brought Kate. Now Kate's life was in jeopardy. What would people say about her as a mother, as a trip leader, if they all died? They'd wonder what kind of person would take others, including her eight-year-old daughter, into such a dangerous place. She tried to take solace from the fact that Kate and the others chose to come along, they wanted to come along and what had happened was not within her control. No matter where they went or what they did, above or below ground, things could happen. Would it be any different if a drunk driver hit the van out on the highway? No matter how careful or safe you were, there were always risks in life. Hadn't the cancer taught her that? She wasn't responsible for the accident, only for making sure they responded the best way they could to the situation. She would love Kate until her last breath, whether that came in hours or decades.

Over and over, like plotting out a chess game strategy, she analyzed their predicament and the question of whether or not to move on. In most cases, if there is a serious problem in a cave, it's best to sit tight and wait to be rescued. But this was not most cases, and there were mitigating factors. She weighed the risks of staying versus the risks of trying to get out through the siphon against each other time and time again. Their supplies were limited, which meant time was of the essence. And if the rescuers needed to chip away or blast the original drop site, they'd be right beneath it if they stayed where they were. The waterfall area was too wet to use as a camp; there they'd be even more susceptible to hypothermia. Their morale and mental status was also something to consider. Danielle knew from experience that sitting and waiting and worrying about a problem usually made it seem much worse. But if they took action—took control of the situation by moving toward freedom—they were more likely to hold their team together and keep fear at bay. Her instincts reassured her that it was worth the risk to move on.

As she stood up straight and threw her shoulders back, she thought she saw an amber light behind her. A warm golden glow as if someone were approaching with a candle. She turned in amazement to find only the ubiquitous darkness. She looked at the others but they were all engrossed in conversation about what missives they would leave. She whirled around again to try to catch a glimpse but there was nothing.

"Hey ya'll, turn on all your lights for a second, over this way," she gestured.

"What is it? What's wrong?" everyone asked as the room was suddenly awash in their lights.

"Nothing's wrong, I just thought I saw a light behind me. It's really weird." She noticed the glances the others were giving her. "Probably just my imagination. Forget I said anything."

"You're seeing things now. Ho boy," Lynne said.

"Maybe it was an angel," Kate said.

"I'd like to think so," Danielle said. "Anyway, it's time for us to move on. According to my watch, it's Sunday morning and time for us to head toward the siphon. Let me scribble down my letter and we'll get going. Has everybody finished theirs? Everyone needs to eat something, too, before we go. If I can borrow your pencil, I'll chow down on one of these gourmet powerbars while I'm writing."

"Can we all leave our lights on for a little while, Mom?" begged Kate. "I like it better like this."

"Just until we finish our letters," Danielle said as she smoothed out the piece of paper Melissa had given her to write on.

Dear Max,

I pray that if somehow this letter ever reaches your hands, I'll already be in your arms telling you in person about this adventure. (Adventure? You can see I'm trying to think positive.) It's Sunday morning and we are heading to the siphon and are going to try and swim through. We don't have enough supplies to wait, even though I know you'll be doing your best to reach us. You'd be proud of Kate and me; we're using everything you taught us and we will get out of here. The rest of the women are doing great, considering. We're all scared but we haven't lost our cool. We're going to leave plenty of trail markers so if someone comes in through the waterfall they can follow our trail. I just pray we can fit through.

Just in case something does happen, I want to ask you: I don't know who pulled up the ropes or caused the cave to collapse, but I do know you; you'll want to take vengeance. Please, please, please don't take that upon yourself. I know you'll be angry but if you retaliate then you'll end up in jail and it won't bring us back. You and I are forever; that means we'll be together long after this life is over. I need you to live out our dream, not be locked up in jail or on the run. If something happens to me and Kate, please build our house on Miracle Ridge. Our spirits will be there with you. Don't risk losing all of that because of what someone else did. I'm counting on you to fulfill our dream. We'll be joined eventually. Live your life out to the fullest; I'll be right there beside you.

I know this will all seem silly when I'm out and laughing and kissing your handsome face again. And believe me, I'll help you rip this letter to shreds and toss it to the wind. I love you, Max.

XXX OOO ♥♥♥ Danielle"

73

Danielle brushed muddy tear stains off the paper and folded it neatly. She placed it on top of the others and sealed them all in the plastic bag. Kate drew a picture of herself (Danielle was glad to see that she'd drawn herself smiling, that was a good sign) and printed the words "open me," which they sealed in another plastic bag and propped strategically on top of the rock-pile for the rescuers to see. She felt that she could write a hundred more pages.

Kate piped up, "Want to know what I wrote?"

Danielle wasn't sure she could handle it, but nodded her assent.

"I just told Daddy that I want to go to Famous Anthony's when we get out of here, and I want to eat a whole Reeses' peanut butter pie."

"Oh no," Gabby said. "Who started talking about food?"

"Not us. We've got work to do," Nicole said. "How 'bout I give you a break and lead for a while, Danielle? I'll take us as far as the waterfall."

"Thanks, Nicole. That'll give me some time to think about how to get us all safely down the cliff. We'll have to get creative with our webbing."

When they reached the cliff, Danielle grimaced. The only way down was vertical, about forty feet, alongside the waterfall. The noise would make communication difficult, and the spray in the air would soak everyone unless they wrapped their hypothermia blankets around them. They'd have to protect themselves or end up dangerously chilled. The entire rock face was wet and slippery; the worst possible climbing conditions. It would be safer with a rope, but no point in wishing.

They had three pieces of thirty-foot one-inch webbing between them that could be tied together with water-knots to reach from the top to the bottom, doubled. Danielle and Nicole finally decided to use Kate's eight, which could also be used to belay. The knots of the webbing would pass through it, but would not through a rack. The webbing wouldn't have nearly the friction of rope, so that could be tricky. They'd have to double wrap it to create enough friction. And, since they didn't know how much webbing they'd need to get through the siphon, they couldn't leave it behind, which added the problem of how to get the last person down the cliff safely.

They began scouting the cliff for the best route and a boulder or formation that Nicole could anchor to with a runner and carabiner as she belayed each one down.

"All of you put your harnesses on. Nicole, you'll need to be really tight on that belay; even with a double wrap, the webbing's going to want to fly through that eight, faster than rope. I'll go down first."

Danielle took a deep breath and squared her shoulders. "It's gonna be weird using webbing but we have no other choice. Listen, you've all had some experience at the climbing wall and at Fools Face, so try to remember what you learned. The thing is, we're going to have to move quickly so we don't get soaked. But move carefully too because the rock is wet." Danielle nodded her head in agreement at the ensuing groans. "It's also going to be hard to hear, as you can tell already, so really shout if you need tension or slack or if something's falling. OK?"

"Why don't we just rappel down?" Gabby said. "Wouldn't it be faster?"

"I thought of that, Gabby, and I'm glad you're thinking about options. Mainly this is to keep the weight off our anchor up here, using it only as a back up rather than having us each put our full weight on it. It seems like a pretty solid formation, but I'm afraid to trust it completely. Stay out of the spray until it's your turn. We'll lower half the packs first. That'll give us a chance to see how well the webbing's going to work in the eight. Once we get them down and half of us, then we'll lower the rest, with Nicole climbing down last. Nicole, one of us will belay you from below. You can run the webbing through the carabiner on that anchor, then we'll just pull the webbing through once you're safely on the bottom, OK? We can afford to leave one runner and carabiner behind. Consider it a trail marker for the rescuers if they get down through the waterfall. Does this plan sound all right to everyone? Is there anything I've forgotten?"

"Mom, I don't want to do this. I want Daddy to be here." Kate began to cry.

"I know, I know. I do too. You've been such a trooper so far, you've got to hang in there a little longer. Do you want to come down right after me?"

"No, I don't want to come down at all," sniffed Kate and broke into fresh tears. She sat down on her cave pack and hid her face in her muddy gloves. Danielle knew her daughter was tired, hungry, and scared like the rest of them. She knew Kate could be stubborn, but didn't blame her after all they'd been through. But this was no time to give up.

"Kate . . ."

"Mom, no!"

"Kate, please sweetie?" Danielle moved toward her.

Gabby moved in between them and knelt down in front of the despondent little girl. She spoke softly, "I have a little boy, just a year older than you." Kate was silent. "His name is Andrew. I've told him all about you." Kate's head was still, but she seemed to be listening. "All about how well you climb and how you go exploring caves with your mom and dad. He's never been in a wild cave."

Kate raised her streaked face, peering at Gabby through stringy hair. "He hasn't?"

"Nope. And he said he sure would like to meet you someday."

"Maybe when we get out," Kate said. The transformation was amazing.

"He'll sure be impressed when he hears about this trip, won't he? So we need to all get out safe and sound so we can tell our friends and families the story, right?"

Kate nodded, then stood and turned toward Danielle. "It's OK mom, I'll do it. But I want to go first."

Danielle sucked in a breath, "First?" She was glad Kate had changed her attitude, but to let her go first? "No, sweetie; that would be too dangerous."

"But I'm a better climber than you, and I'm lighter too."

Danielle couldn't argue with either fact, but eight years' worth of motherhood still outweighed both arguments in her mind. Flashbacks of Kate's tiny body on the scales minutes after she was born, eyes wide to take in the new world around her; the flurry of toddler years exploring and reading bedtime stories together every night; the infinite times she'd hugged her in wonder and love.

Danielle had looked at Kate in awe as she seemed to grow an inch taller right before her eyes.

"Yes, you are, but . . ."

"But what?"

"Something might happen."

"Oh right. We're trapped in a cave and climbing down cliffs and going to have to swim through a tunnel nobody's ever been through before, and you're worried something might happen? Mom! Think about what you're saying."

"She's right," interrupted Gabby.

"You're going to have to trust her," Melissa said. "I've seen her climb and I think she can do it. It'll give us a chance to see how the webbing works without the weight of one of us adults on it. You said yourself that we shouldn't put any more weight on it than we have to. We're all going down there anyway; she won't be alone for long. You can climb down right after her."

"I can do it, Mom. Please?"

Danielle lifted her hands helplessly. Deep down, she knew Kate would be all right. She was just so afraid to let go. A small voice whispered that it wouldn't be over even when they got out; there were all the other stepping stones of growing up that stretched out before Kate; schools and peer pressure, puppy love, getting a driver's license, dating in the world of AIDS. She had to learn to trust Kate's abilities.

"Well, okay. I wasn't thinking about how we'd get the packs untied at the bottom anyway. Will you do that for us, please?"

They made sure Kate's harness was secure and agreed to turn on most of their lights during the climbing process. It would be hard enough to get good footing with the waterfall spray everywhere without having to do it in dim light. Nicole put the webbing in the eight and brought the brake-tail around behind her. Danielle sat near the edge where she could watch Kate's progress. She kept swallowing to keep her heart out of her throat.

"Hey Gabby, would you do me a favor?" Kate said. "Would you take my picture? I want to show Andrew that I was the first one down."

"Sure, kid." Gabby pulled out the camera and clicked a shot of Kate's proud grin. She had one picture left on the roll. She was saving that one for the other side.

Danielle admired Kate's grace and flexibility as the young girl moved confidently down the wall, keeping her center of gravity over whichever foot was bearing her weight. Kate paused briefly at a few places where the slant of the wall tried to throw her off balance, but like a little cave cricket she deftly made her way down the cliff, and arrived at the bottom with barely a slip.

The women let out a cheer when they heard Kate's strong voice yell up, "Off rope!"

"She's really something," Danielle said in utter relief.

"*Alis volat propriis*," Nicole smiled. "She flies with her own wings."

Danielle gave Kate a thumbs up and blew her a kiss. Another lesson learned. Now if she could only do as well.

"How'd that eight do with the webbing? She didn't put her whole weight on it, could you tell?"

"Well, let's tie three of the packs on there and see how it does." Danielle tied the packs on using in-line butterfly knots. The packs were lowered successfully to Kate who untied them without a hitch.

It was Danielle's turn. Despite the fact that she was being belayed, Danielle didn't want to stress the system. She'd have to climb as if she had no protection at all, as if she were free soloing. She managed a brave wave and began her descent. Kate had made it look so easy, but she quickly found it wasn't. The footholds seemed to reject her boots, and handholds her wet gloves. She talked to herself the whole way.

She didn't want to look down . . . or up. She wanted to close her eyes and make it all go away. She wanted to be somewhere else. Anywhere else. Balance was the key. One step at a time, simultaneously keeping an overall picture of her destination. Getting off route could make all those little steps fruitless.

Balance. Everything in life was a balance. Passion with dependability. Working with playing. Inhaling with exhaling. The big picture with details. Her body with the cliff. She could almost hear Max's voice whispering in her ear, "Don't fight the rock, work with it. Read it." She was sweating with concentration. A few more moves and then finally, she was down. Kate embraced her and helped her untie the webbing. In unison they hollered upward, "Off rope." Danielle was panting with relief.

One by one the women made the arduous descent.

At last only Nicole remained. Danielle knew this would be a tremendous challenge for Nicole. She also knew the last thing Nicole wanted was to be alone at the top. Her desire to be with the rest of the women would carry her down.

They all waved and shouted support. It took Nicole a while to get over the edge. She was trying not to put her total weight on the webbing. Gradually she descended. Danielle climbed vicariously with her from the bottom, ready to brake her at any second. Things were going well until Nicole started moving away from the waterfall to an inviting ledge. Danielle remembered it as a spot where she had been thrown off balance, and became concerned as Nicole continued to the left, rather than straight down. If she continued at that angle and fell, she would pendulum—swing—and possibly get hurt.

"Nicole, move back over to the right," Danielle called out.

But Nicole couldn't hear her above the water noise, or was concentrating so hard the words meant nothing. She continued following the larger ledge to the left.

"Nicole, get back to the right!"

"But there's nothing to put my feet on over there," answered Nicole finally, her voice quaking.

"I know it's not much, but it's too dangerous where you are. Get back to the right!"

"I can't. Just let me come down this way a little more," Nicole pleaded.

And then her toes slipped off the slippery sloping ledge. They watched, horrified and helpless as Nicole gyrated across the jagged face of the cliff. She screamed and her free arm came up across her face instinctively as she slammed against the unyielding rocks. Danielle kept the belay line tight from below. Then Nicole rolled back to the left, and finally came to a stop. Most of her movement had been horizontal; Danielle's quick reflexes had prevented her from dropping very far. Thankfully, the anchor was holding topside.

"Nicole! Nicole, are you OK? We've got to get you down."

Danielle was afraid to stress the system further, it had already received the shock-load of Nicole's weight.

"Help me!" Nicole cried over the waterfall's roar.

"We're going to lower you Nicole, walk it down, just do it like you're rappelling."

"I hurt my arm!"

"The quicker we get you down, the better. We're lowering you, Nicole. Come on."

Together they got her down and gently laid her on her back. The helmet had protected her head but a sharp, pointed rock had gashed her right arm, right through her sleeve. There was so much blood seeping out, Danielle couldn't tell right away if any bones were broken. She knew she had to stop the bleeding and keep Nicole from going into shock. She pulled her muddy gloves off and pulled on a pair of the disposable ones that Lynne found in Nicole's medical kit. She pressed her hand firmly against the area where most of the blood seemed to be coming from. Melissa removed Nicole's helmet, murmuring to Nicole to lie still. She then pulled the bandanna from around her head and handed it to Danielle to use as a compress. Lynne raised Nicole's knees and shoved one of their packs under them to keep them elevated. The smell of Nicole's warm blood rose to meet them.

"This bandanna's so dirty—hurry up and get some water out, somebody, and pull a clean compress out of that kit. Hurry."

"Is it broken?" moaned Nicole. She was starting to shiver in spite of the hypothermia blanket. "Don't let me pass out, keep pressure on it, stop the bleeding."

"Just hold still," Danielle said. "Get some of those heat packs out, Sydney, and put them in the bag with her. Let's stop the bleeding first. Nicole, can you feel your fingers? Try to wiggle them just a little for me."

"How bad is it?" Nicole was quieter now, but still ashen. Kate picked up Nicole's other hand, holding it reassuringly. "It feels hot; but look . . ." and the delicate fingers curled in against the palm and out again, as if grasping for reassurance.

Danielle slowly released her pressure against the arm and lifted the blood-soaked bandanna. They carefully pulled back the sleeve to expose the wound. It was an ugly laceration, quite deep, but didn't appear to go to the bone. Sydney pulled out a canteen so she and Lynne could wash their hands and then both of them put on disposable gloves. Lynne volunteered to take over saying she'd had plenty of experience with the boo-boo's of three kids.

They washed the torn flesh as well as they could, following Nicole's orders to irrigate the wound with some of the drinking water that hadn't been opened yet.

Nicole supervised their every step and when it was obvious the steri-strips weren't going to hold the gaping wound together, especially during the exertions she'd be facing, she winced, "You're going to have to stitch it."

"With what?" Sydney said.

"There's a miniature suture kit in my bag there. Lynne, see if you can find it. It's got a pre-packed curved needle and some prolene, nylon thread in there. You'll need . . . Ow! . . . it hurts . . . you'll need the hemostats too. Do you know what they look like?"

Nicole closed her eyes against the pain.

"Got 'em," Lynne said.

"Can you do this?" Sydney said. "I hate needles."

"I've watched my kids get stitched up in the ER many times. And I'm a great seamstress," Lynne said. "Hey, I'm a mom with three rowdy kids. Ya'll know I've got to be good at patching things up. Which color do you want? Black or blue? Here, the blue will match your coveralls."

"Dear Lord, it hurts. Either one, blue's fine."

Nicole took a deep breath and examined the wound again. "You're going to have to trim the edges a little first. Use those surgical scissors. Think you can handle this?"

"Here goes. It'll hurt." Lynne bent to her task and paused each time Nicole cried out in pain. "I'm sorry," she said.

"No, no. Keep going. You've almost got it ready. Check it once more to make sure there's no dirt or grit in the wound." Nicole looked away as Sydney flushed the area again with the clean water.

Following Nicole's instructions, Lynne used the hemostats to pull the curved P1 needle though the skin. She tied off each stitch with a square knot.

"Right over left, left over right," Lynne whispered as she tied the nylon thread. Beads of sweat shone on her forehead and upper lip.

"If I had my sewing machine, I could give you a monogram," Lynne said as she tied off another stitch.

"Don't make me laugh . . . it hurts. No matter how much I yell or beg you to stop, keep going until you get it sewed up."

And yell she did. Kate covered her ears, then began rummaging in her pack. "You can have my last candy bar."

"Thanks Kate, but you hold onto it. You can help, though. Look in my stuff there for some antibiotics I'll need to take. It says 'cefadroxil, 500 mg,' on it. Give me two of them to start with." In spite of the pain she was able to continue instructing Lynne with amazing clarity; the wound received nine simple stitches. Kate watched the whole operation, fascinated, and let Nicole squeeze her hand when the waves of pain washed over her. Then, they applied a good measure of the triple antibiotic ointment over Lynne's handiwork, and double-checked for any other injuries.

Aside from a few bruises and tender spots, there seemed to be no other serious damage. "I'm sorry you got hurt, but at least it's your arm and not your pretty face," said Melissa softly, touching Nicole's cheek.

Nicole lay back and managed a grin at Lynne, "Fine work, lady."

Lynne smiled weakly. Now that it was over, she was feeling queasy, and gratefully let the others minister to the patient while she got a grip on herself. It was the same with her children; when they fell out of a tree or busted open their knee wrecking their bicycle, she could take charge without any thought to her own emotions. Get them to the hospital, comfort them while waiting for the doctor, make small talk to keep them distracted while the hospital staff tended to the injuries, and get the prescriptions filled on the way home. Once it was all over, she'd sequester herself in the bathroom and let the sobs flow. The tears came now.

Their main concern was to keep Nicole warm. And although their supplies were dwindling fast, they knew they had to get enough nourishment into Nicole to combat shock and chills. The full force of the pain would catch up with her once the initial trauma of the accident wore off.

82

Danielle let Sydney take charge of Nicole's care, talking to her, feeding her, and getting her warm, while she and Melissa followed the stream around the bend. She was relieved for the opportunity to get away from the cliff for a breather. It had taken its toll on them.

Their conversation stilled at the sight of what lay below them. The stream disappeared beneath a mountain of jumbled breakdown. Danielle and Melissa leaned against each other. How would they ever get through that? And what about Nicole? There were gaping holes in the rocks, but would they be able to finagle their way through?

Melissa began poking her head into some of the various nooks and crannies, and suddenly stood up and said, "I'll lead us through. I think I see a way."

"Are you sure? I've never been through this section myself."

"I don't know how to explain it, Danielle, I just feel like I'm supposed to lead us through this part. I feel like it's meant to be. Let me be navigator."

"I'm too tired to argue. If you're sure . . ."

Melissa smiled, "I'm sure. Trust me."

They returned to the others, relieved to find Nicole sitting up and eating tiny pieces of powerbar Kate was pinching off for her. They could see the color back in her face, and her arm was bound up snugly in a sling to keep it close to her body.

"There's more fun ahead," Melissa said, describing the obstacle.

"Look, this hurts like hell," Nicole said, "but I think we ought to do it now, before the adrenaline wears off. If ya'll will help me, I'd just as soon do it now and rest when I get to the other side. Just pump me up with about four of those 200 mg ibuprofen and let's do it."

Danielle knelt at Nicole's side. "Do you think you can do this? We don't know how long it will take to find our way through that stuff."

"I don't care. I just want to do it while I still can."

They rechecked Nicole's pupils and pulse and, convinced she was oriented enough to make such a decision, gathered up their packs and headed for the breakdown. They took turns carrying Nicole's pack and leading her along.

"Just let me say one thing before we start crawling through this stuff," Danielle said. "If you've ever played 'Jinga' blocks or 'pick up sticks,' that's what this looks like. If you move or bump the wrong rock, the whole thing could shift and collapse. We have to move through like a mother trying not to wake a baby from its nap. Don't even breathe hard. If you have to sneeze or cough, for heaven's sake, do it now."

"What if we get the hiccups, Mom?"

"Kate, I'm in no mood to joke. This is serious. Use common sense. Move slowly, deliberately, but don't stay in one place too long either. And Melissa, if something looks too shaky, don't risk it."

"If you can, try to keep track of the stream, too," Sydney said. "We want to end up at the siphon, not a dead end."

They began their undulations through the labyrinth. Melissa seemed to have found a viable route, and they made slow but steady progress. Nicole was running on a kind of miraculous high, determination fueling her onward despite the excruciating pain in her arm. She insisted on continuing, even though her grunts and whimpers told the rest that the pain must be agonizing.

"What's wrong?" Danielle whispered when everything came to a halt. Not daring to raise her voice but knowing the message would get passed up and then answered the same way.

"Melissa said she has to back up a little," said Kate. "It's okay now. She found a way through."

Danielle waited, and finally they were moving again. She focused on one movement at a time. Like climbing at North Carolina's Stone Mountain; one step at a time. Would she ever climb that beautiful granite giant again? Stick her climbing shoes to the friction and move up its 640 feet like a human fly? You could see forever from up there. The multicolored quilt of piedmont and farmlands below. A kettle of hawks boiling above and a tiny orange ladybug landing on her forearm.

She couldn't believe Nicole's perseverance. Like a dog sled crossing an ice-covered lake, or soldiers tip-toeing through a minefield, they wound their way through the precarious boulders. They all wanted so badly to be through with this crawl, but rushing would be suicidal. It was a slow, painstaking process. Danielle admired Melissa's choice of route.

"Finally. It's opening up. I'm through!" Melissa shouted, and it was all the rest of them could do to keep from rushing forward heedlessly to reach the same reward. But reward was a relative term, for there below them yawned the siphon.

8

Piece of Cake

Jake pounded on the screen door again. The banging echoed the pounding pain in his head. He finally heard movements in the back of the house.

"BJ, open up. I know you're in there." He shook the flimsy wooden door again, tempted to rip it off its hinges.

"Who is it?"

"You know damn well who it is, open up." Jake rattled the door again until finally he saw BJ approaching warily.

BJ leaned against the inside of the door, but didn't unhook the latch. His arm was in a cast, his fingers swollen and purple.

"I've been trying to call you for hours. How come you wouldn't answer your phone? What did they say when you called?" Jake squinted through the screen at BJ, still waiting for him to open the door.

"I was in the ER most of the night," BJ said. "Then they gave me some stuff for the pain."

"So what time was it when you called 911?" Jake was starting to panic.

"That stuff knocked me on my ass. I was out cold 'til you woke me up."

"Damn it, BJ," groaned Jake, "you didn't call, did you?" He

slammed his fist against the door and spun away, then whirled back again, ready to knock the door down.

"Well, by the time the doc got the cast on and . . ."

"Tim's still in the cave. So are the . . . they've been in there all night."

"They were asking too many questions at the hospital. I'm in enough deep shit as it is. You and I know this whole damn thing was an accident, but they might not see it that way."

"God, I thought it was bad before," Jake said. "I should've known you'd pull something like this. I should've made sure you called for help before I even dropped you off at the emergency room." He grabbed the door handle. "Let me use your phone."

"No way. They could trace the call."

"Damn you! I'll do it. You'd better hope I'm not too late." Jake ran across the lawn to his car to find the nearest pay phone.

Later, leaning against his Shenandoah County Sheriff's car, Jackson Lee mopped his sweaty forehead with an already soggy handkerchief as he waited for reinforcements. He hitched his pants up over his large belly and absently rested his hand on the butt of his pistol. He twitched as some sweat ran down from his armpit. Could use some rain to cool things down, he thought. The radio blared static. An anonymous call had come in that morning: someone was hurt in Dragons Den cave and needed help. It could just be some teenagers playing a prank, but he was required to check it out, regardless. There had been something urgent and painful about the caller's voice; it could be a bona fide emergency. The caller had also started to say something else, but then seemed to change his mind and hung up abruptly before the Sheriff could get any more details.

By the time the Sheriff had arranged for his Deputy and two back-ups to meet him at the cave entrance it was past noon. Church traffic held him up a bit, but now he was here scratching his bald head and wondering if kids caused trouble like this as pay-back for his own wilder days. He scanned the woods around the entrance cliff, willing the unfortunate victim to come stumbling out of his own accord. Oh well, his deputy was green and enthusiastic; he'd probably relish a Sunday afternoon adventure. There was no way the Sheriff himself was venturing into any dark, damp hole in the

ground. But Sam and a few of his fire fighter buddies would probably appreciate getting out of the July heat.

Sam pulled up behind the Sheriff's car, followed by Rod and Buddy, two of the county's more gung-ho fire fighters. Rod had a rope slung over his shoulder. All were in coveralls. They wore hard hats with lamps on them, and carried large heavy-duty flashlights.

"Any of you ever been in this cave before?" Sheriff Lee said, slugging down a lukewarm cola and unwrapping a stick of gum. (What he really wanted was a cigarette, but, he'd been feeling his mortality lately and figured he'd better quit.)

"I went once back in high school," Buddy said. "We'll find 'em. 'Piece of cake."

"Yeah, thanks, Lee. It's hot as hell out here; the cave will feel good; nice and cool. This is almost as good as bustin' skinny-dippers down at the Blue Hole."

"The sun has definitely fried your brain, Sam," Buddy said. If that's what you do all summer long I think I'll apply for your job."

"Who are we lookin' for, Lee?" Sam said, anxious to get it all over with and get back home where the family was waiting to grill burgers and toss some horseshoes.

"Well, we got an anonymous call saying that some fellow named Tim is hurt in there and needs to be carried out. I've put in a call to the local cave rescue folks, but while we're waiting on them to get here, I want ya'll to go on in and assess the situation. For one thing, I'm not sure this isn't a prank call. And for another, we don't need to be bringing in a whole contingent of outside folks if we can take care of this thing locally. You three go in there and check it out. If this guy is hurt, help him out if his injuries aren't serious; if he's in bad shape, do what you can to stabilize him until the others get here. At least we'll be able to show them where he is."

"Any idea who made the call?"

"I have some suspicions, but we'll address that later. We need to get in there fast in case someone really is hurt."

"Right. You got an extra flashlight and a blanket? I was in such a hurry to get here I didn't bring much."

Jackson grabbed his police flashlight and a woolen blanket from the back seat and tossed it to Sam.

"Listen. It's after one now. It shouldn't take you more than a couple hours. Make sure you're back here by 3:00, whether you locate the guy or not."

"We'll find him. If he's in there, we'll find him," Buddy said. "I sure don't plan on spending all day hanging out with bats and chasing down cave rats when I've got grilled hamburgers and iced watermelon waiting for me at home."

"Want to adopt a poor hungry firefighter?" Sam chuckled.

Rod started walking toward the cave entrance impatiently. "Come on!"

As they were leaving, Sheriff Lee got a call on the radio to break up a domestic disturbance. He promised to be back before 3:00, then left, squealing his tires. The three men scrambled their way up to the cave entrance.

9

Orchestration of a Rescue

Max jumped out of his truck and was joined by a carload of Grotto members. Sheriff Lee looked up. His three boys were lying in various exhausted positions in the tall roadside weeds. Sam was nursing a sprained ankle and all three were pale and shivering despite the torrid July heat.

Max walked up to the Sheriff and shook hands. "We got your call. I'm Max Stewart with Triangle Cave Rescue and the Big Lick Grotto. Did you locate the women? And the man who was reportedly hurt? Are all your men okay?"

"We can show you where the injured party, Tim, is. But what women? We didn't know about any women in the cave. The caller just told us about the one guy. I don't see any other cars nearby."

Max drew a deep breath to control his mounting fear, "My wife and daughter and five women went in to spend the night in the cave and were supposed to have called me when they got out. My wife knows the cave owner so she probably parked down the road at his place. They had a call-back time of 5:00 p.m. today. When I got your call for help, I assumed something had gone wrong, even though it isn't 5:00 yet."

"You let your wife and daughter go in there?" The Sheriff reached for his gum. It looked to him as though today was going to be another one of those three-packer days.

Ignoring the Sheriff's accusatory tone, Max said, "They're both experienced cavers, and so was the other trip leader." He turned to the three men resting in the grass. "Did you see any women? Where is this guy, Tim? Is anyone taking care of him now? Is he still alive?"

"We wrapped a blanket around him, but to be honest, we thought it would be wiser to let you guys carry him out." Buddy had lost his cocksure manner. "His leg looked pretty bad. We were able to revive him for a few minutes but he wasn't making much sense. Between Sam's busted ankle and that guy's bum leg, we were afraid we'd do more harm than good. And I'm sorry but we didn't see any women."

"We did see a bunch of camping gear and sleeping bags in one area," Sam said.

"In the Dragon's Dining Room?"

"I don't know what you call it. But it was a bunch of stuff; sleeping bags, duffel bags . . ."

"That's where they planned to spend the night. You didn't see any women at all?"

"No sir. That is one big cave."

"What about at the drop to the lower level?"

"Drop? We saw all kinds of holes and pits. But I'm not sure about any lower level," Sam said.

"You'd know if you saw it, it's a hundred-foot drop."

"Do you know what he's talking about, Buddy? We didn't fall in any hundred foot holes today, although it felt like it!"

Buddy shook his head and rolled up his pants legs to check his bruised knees.

"What about that pink stuff?" prompted Sam, gesturing to Rob with a dirty index finger.

"Pink stuff . . . webbing?" Max jumped at a possible clue.

Rob pulled a piece of hot pink webbing out of his pocket. It was muddy and frayed at one end. "We did find this somewhere back past their camping area. Near where we found Tim."

Max unrolled his map of Dragons Den and asked Buddy to point to where he had found Tim and the webbing.

"Why didn't you leave it where it was so we'd have some idea of where to look for them?" asked Max. Even so, he knew the general area of the drop they planned to use. The webbing was in pieces; he wondered if something had gone wrong with the anchors.

"I'm sorry; I didn't think about that. I don't know anything about this caving stuff. We were just trying to help."

Max knew Danielle used that kind of webbing. He doubted the guy who was hurt would use the same color, if he used webbing at all.

"Sheriff," he said, "I'm going to send in a team to pull Tim out of there, and initiate a full rescue to search for the women. Do you have any other information about Tim, or the caller? Do you have any idea if they would have messed with other people in the cave? With the women if they ran into them?" Max felt the answer before he heard it. The Sheriff's hesitation and anxious eyes said it all.

"Since you're the legislated authority," Max went on, "you're the Incident Commander. We'll supply the manpower since we have a whole network of cavers who are familiar with the cave. The guy heading toward us right now, Ernie, will assist you. He's with Triangle Cave Rescue and . . ."

"Stop right there," the Sheriff raised his hand in protest, "I'll pass on the 'Commander' part. I'll stay here on the scene and help any way I know how, but as far as coordinating the rescue in the cave, I'd rather delegate that to this Ernie fellow if you don't mind. We're pretty short-handed these days and I may get other calls that require my presence."

"No problem. Ernie knows exactly what to do, and any help you can give him would be greatly appreciated." Max hid his relief at being able to put Ernie in charge. But he had to be diplomatic; they were on the Sheriff's turf.

"And Sheriff," Max said, "thanks for calling us when you did."

"No problem." He glanced at Max's strained face, "I hope your wife's all right. How old is your little girl?"

Max swallowed the lump in his throat, "Eight." The look in his eyes warned the Sheriff to get on with the job at hand.

Ernie sent in an Initial Response Team (IRT-1) to begin

emergency medical procedures on Tim while the Extrication Team worked its way in with the stretcher. Max and five Grotto members formed the second IRT (IRT-2), whose sole purpose was to head for the back of the cave to search for the women. They would call out and scan the area as they blitzed through; and since four of them knew the cave intimately, they could hit the most likely areas.

Danielle. Kate. Max shook his head and tried to remain objective. If he let his emotions override his actions he'd end up getting hurt too, and how would that help his family? Because the piece of webbing had been found near Tim, Max decided to head that way with IRT-2 so he could question him. If he was with it enough to answer questions, he might give them the exact location of the women. If not, Max would leave Tim with IRT-1 and take his team deeper into the cave.

With a hasty prayer, Max and both IRT's disappeared into the cave entrance, leaving Ernie in charge as Incident Commander. Ernie had years of experience with cave rescues and was well respected by members of both Triangle Cave Rescue and the Grotto.

Ernie assigned two recently arrived cavers as Entrance Control. Clipboards in hand, they stayed at the entrance of the cave and kept a detailed log of everyone who entered and exited: Name, date, time in, time out, affiliation, and a list of any equipment.

Four other cavers were appointed Underground Control. They would work closely with the IC, from within the cave. The Communications Team was responsible for running the telephone lines from UC to the IC. They kept in constant contact with each other—reporting what they found (or didn't find) and relaying any information or equipment/manpower needs to the surface. The field phones were heavy, and the lines had to be kept connected as they moved deeper into the cave. One of the UC members also kept a detailed diary of these communications. This prevented mix-ups, and might be needed later if litigation was involved.

A Sweep Team was on stand-by, pending what Max and the IRT could find out from Tim. If he couldn't tell them where the women were, the Sweep Team would start a thorough search of every nook and cranny, beginning at the entrance and working toward the back. Once IRT-2 reached the back of the cave, if they hadn't located the patients (as they would now be called), they would turn around and become a Sweep Team too and work from the back to the front. One or the other team should find the patients somewhere in between.

The Sweep Team and the IRT's would each send a pair of runners to report to the UC every few hours, or if anything significant was found. This information was recorded and reported to the IC over the field phones. Ernie could then send in fresh volunteers, equipment, and commands as appropriate.

Ernie also had a Logistics Team on the outside to bring in food, drinks, and equipment for volunteers and to work with the local paramedics and sheriff's people. There was an Information Officer to deal with the media when it got wind of the rescue, and a Chief Medical Officer whose team would take care of the rescuers as well as the patients. Ernie had a tremendous job synchronizing and directing the big picture. He had once remarked to Max that he felt like he was in the middle of a Where's Waldo cartoon.

The two IRT's flew through the cave toward the area where they felt Tim would most likely be found. As they went, they called out and paused at intervals to listen for any sounds of him or the women. At the Dragon's Dining Room they scanned the camping gear. All was organized, no signs of a problem there. They continued on toward the drop, the site of the accident according to Sam.

The picture of his wife and daughter was so strong in Max's mind that he felt they were okay, but in some kind of jeopardy. He ached to hear that familiar voice calling, "Daddy!" and knew Danielle would be doing her best to hold the group together if it was in danger. She was stronger than she thought she was. His senses, intensified by the search, picked up the odor of beer. "Damn!" He pushed on harder, urging the rest of the team to be safe but move fast. If he found that this Tim guy had deliberately hurt his family, he'd be awfully tempted to make sure it was a body recovery rather than a rescue.

Just before they reached the area of the drop, one of the IRT members spotted the man's feet sticking out of a passageway. "Max, I found him. I can't tell yet if he's breathing." Working quickly they got Tim out and found a slight pulse at his neck. It was obvious his leg had been badly broken, and hypothermia was threatening to snuff him out permanently, despite the blanket wrapped around him by the Sheriff's men. While two IRT-1 members stuffed heat packs under his arms, in his groin and near his torso, and wrapped a space blanket around him to warm him up, Max and the others searched the area looking for clues.

Max's heart nearly stopped when he saw the pile of rocks where the pit had been. He wanted to throw himself against those rocks and pick them up, one by one, like Hercules. Tucker, a friend from the Grotto, put a gloved hand on Max's shoulder.

"Max, come here. He's trying to talk."

Max knelt stiffly by the man who was, in all likelihood, responsible for his wife's entrapment.

"What's your name?"

". . . Ti . . . Tim."

"Tim, tell me what happened."

"I . . . I have to save her . . . have to."

"Save who?" Max grabbed Tim's head to hold it steady.

"I told them . . . not to. I should have . . . stopped them."

"Stopped who? Tim, help us for God's sake. Save who?" Max was getting desperate but was helpless to force it out of Tim any faster.

"I have to save Lynne . . . tell her I'm . . ."

"Was Lynne in the lower level? With other women?"

"BJ . . . and Jake . . . we heard women in the bottom . . . they pulled up the ropes . . . we were gonna put 'em back . . . I swear."

Although Tim's blue-lipped pallor hinted that he might not make it, Max pulled him roughly up to his face and shouted, "What? What did you do?"

"I'm sorry . . ." Tim's voice came out in a raw whisper.

"Sorry? Is that all you can say?"

"Max!" Tucker said. "Chill out. Come over here for a minute." He pulled Max away. "You need to find out everything you can from this guy. Go easy." After a couple of dry swallows, Max said, "You're right. I'm OK now, I won't do anything stupid." He returned to Tim, straining to listen.

"I told 'em not to do it. We were gonna put the ropes back."

"Where are BJ and Jake now?" Max said.

"They were climbing . . . everything started falling. They must be underneath it all. A boulder landed on my leg but I dug myself out . . . to try to get help. Please . . . help me get Lynne out. I have to tell her . . . Just get her out." Tim closed his eyes in exhaustion.

Max walked away, clenching and unclenching his fists. He glared at the rocks that covered the hole. Tim thought his friends were dead. How would he feel when he learned his two buddies deserted him? At least one of them called for help.

Max and Tucker quickly began the trip back to Underground Control who would have Communications phone the news out to the entrance. The Extrication Team arrived and began packaging Tim for transport out of the cave. Max and Tucker continued on to the surface. The remaining members of the IRT's and the Sweep Team would join the Extrication Team to assist in getting Tim out. More volunteers were on their way as well.

Max barely noticed his trip out of the cave. He was too busy thinking about the lay of the cave and all the possible options for access to the lower level.

Outside, Max stripped off his sweat-soaked caving coveralls and dropped his helmet and gloves to the ground. Sheriff Lee offered him refuge in the squad car, which had been moved as close to Ernie's command post as possible. A faint flash of lightening pulsated in the distant sky and leaves were turning their bellies upward in anticipation of an approaching storm. Max wiped his face with the back of his arm, tears and perspiration stinging his eyes. Buddy handed him a soda and a fried chicken breast.

Max forced himself to think about the technical problems of the rescue. To try to get to the lower level through the new, unstable breakdown would be dangerous for the women below as well as for the rescuers above. He thought about the low stream passage to the top of the waterfall. No one had ever gotten in that way, but perhaps the passage could be enlarged. That might be quicker and safer than trying to get through the original drop.

The waterfall plummeted about a hundred feet, then flowed through the cave into a siphon, and, according to the Grotto's survey and dye tracing, out the resurgence. Although they'd visited the siphon from both sides, no one had ever felt it worth the effort of a dive.

"Max, I don't suppose it'd do any good to tell you to try and get some rest, would it?" Max gazed stonily at Ernie, who continued, "You did one hell of a job with the IRT. How 'bout helping me out up here as Chief of Operations and Planning? As I'm sure you know, this is no longer a simple rescue. We're going to have to pull in dynamiters and divers, and figure out a way to get to those women fast. This weather isn't going to help us either."

"I appreciate it, Ernie. I'd dive that siphon myself if . . ."

"That's precisely why I want you in charge of O&P. I know that's your wife and daughter in there, and I can imagine how anxious you are to get to them. But I also know you want to be where you can help the most, and not compromise the rescue by taking dangerous risks."

Max slowly nodded his assent.

"Good man," Ernie said. "What's your game plan? Do you have anyone in particular in mind?"

"I know a good local dynamiter: Ashby Thompson. I'll try him first and have him look at the breakdown over the drop. The passage to the waterfall too, to see if we couldn't widen it and get through there. I'll also call Mariah from the Big Lick Grotto and have her get some cave divers."

"Good. I'll have a couple of cavers standing by to lead in the dynamite team and dive team when they arrive, and I'll keep enough rescuers available to help when we get to the patients. Let me know when you've lined your folks up."

Max sat in the open doorway of the Sheriff's car, punching in the numbers on the cellular phone and massaging his neck, vaguely listening to thunder grumble on the other side of the mountain. Lightening ripped the sky just at the moment they brought Tim out, wrapped up and packaged in the sked stretcher like a mummy. The Media Officer and Sheriff Lee kept the reporters at bay. Tim was whisked away in an ambulance, but the fatigue and sadness in the cavers' eyes told Max that Tim probably wouldn't make it. Max made a mental note to make sure Ernie had arranged for counseling for the members of the extrication team who might have problems dealing with the news that their patient expired despite the rescue. He himself felt no pity for this person who had put his family in danger.

The line to Ashby was busy.

A TV crew struggled to get sensationalistic shots of the tired cavers retreating from the storm to the rehabilitation area where they would get fed, warmed, and have any medical problems cared for. Away from the probing camera lights, Max questioned Tucker, "Did he say anything else?"

"He opened his eyes for just a second, and yelled, 'I'm coming, Lynne.' Then he passed out."

Max looked up at the heavy clouds roiling in. The storm arrived with such force that the wind stripped leaves from the trees, and the sky turned so black he might as well have been back in the cave.

10

Hold Your Breath

There was no escaping the darkness. It wrapped around them like a damp heavy blanket and seeped into their every pore. Requests to turn on a light were coming more frequently and urgently.

"Wait just a little longer," Danielle said. "We've got to stretch out the life of the few batteries we have left."

It had taken them all of Sunday to make their way to the siphon. They agreed unanimously to give their bodies a rest and wait until the next morning to attempt the swim.

They inventoried the remaining food by the light of a glow-stick, and Nicole supervised the making of warm drinks, leaving one last batch for just before Monday morning's cold swim. They took turns telling stories as they let the warmth of the liquid spread through their tired bodies. Their tales took on a radiance as they used carefully chosen words and inflections to make up for the gestures and facial expressions that couldn't be seen in the darkness.

As Danielle wrapped her hands around her warm mug, her thoughts gyrated in all directions. This was how she imagined it felt to be a fetus in a womb. Except it was warm there and now she was shivering cold. A baby has the heartbeat and body sounds of its mother to rock it rhythmically, to remind it that it was not alone. Danielle could hear her own heart pumping determinedly, and she was glad to smell the scent of the other women nearby and hear their soft words and sounds. We're like seven little babies in the belly of this great dragon, she thought.

Danielle's hand went subconsciously to her belly as she remembered how Kate had grown within her. About eight months along into her pregnancy, she'd lie on her back in bed and watch her tummy rise and swell with the child's somersaults. Letting her hands rest gently on her tautly stretched abdomen, she could feel the hard head and insistent little elbows and feet of her unborn child press and push mightily, stretching and growing. The baby would often get the hiccups and Danielle couldn't help but giggle every time she felt the little spasms inside of her. She loved the feeling of being with child, of carrying that precious miracle near her heart.

That was over eight years ago. Was she growing old as fast as Kate was growing up? Now that was a sobering thought. But it wasn't the growing older that scared her as much as the thought of her allotment of time running out prematurely. There were so many things she wanted to do and see before making the ultimate journey.

She wondered what the people back at the office would say if she were to die in the cave. They thought she was crazy anyway; they'd seen the pictures on her bulletin board of Murder Hole, of Max straddling the summit of Seneca Rocks, Kate rappelling into Murder Hole, and Danielle and her friends from the Grotto covered with mud after a trip into James Cave. She had to admit she seemed to lead an impossible number of lives. On weekdays she churned out graphs and charts in the Quality Management department of the VA hospital. Her job was to track and trend the progress of the bureaucracy, a phrase she sometimes considered an oxymoron. Weeknights were spent with Max and Kate, squeezing in artwork and music between loads of laundry and helping Kate with her homework. Weekends were spent out on Miracle Ridge or helping Max lead climbing and caving trips.

She'd done a drawing once of all her different shoes: muddy caving boots, colorful climbing shoes called Flashdances, cream-colored Victorian lace-up boots, black and red cowgirl boots, running shoes, and sexy silver high-heels. Looking at each pair separately, she couldn't imagine giving up any one of them. They were all intertwined with her artwork and music, her family, her job, and the road of life she was traveling.

She hoped her parents wouldn't get wind of her present situation until she and the team were safely above ground. She never could quite tell exactly how they felt about this adventurous life of hers. Perhaps her father would understand her hunger for challenges. He had always been an adventurer and nonconformist: scuba diving, parachuting, and inventing things. He worked as an aeronautical engineer for NASA, but his innovative mind and exuberant ideas were often too much even for his coworkers to comprehend. He and Danielle told each other about the frustrations and small victories that came from working for the government. She knew well whose genes had instilled in her the determination to fight for what was right whenever issues arose, although sometimes she wondered if it was a blessing or a curse.

She was the eldest of five children, and had been her father's fishing buddy during her early years. He'd roust her out of bed at 5 a.m. and they'd head for Lake Lanier, north of Atlanta. One of her favorite pictures was of herself at the age of five struggling to hold up a 5-pound large-mouth bass and a 3-pound small-mouth bass, while her father held up two little minnows. He'd stuck his bottom lip out as if to pout, but she'd known he was proud of her.

Her father and her grandfather, Gramps, had taken her on hikes near her grandparents' home in Alabama. Once they'd taken her to a quarry where she'd found a fossil of a fish in the shale and listened to Gramps preach about the Great Flood. Not just any flood, Noah's. Somehow on the hike back, she'd lost the rock, and searched tearfully for it until her father said it was time to get on home. "Just leave it be," Gramps had said. She still felt a small bit of loss; as young as she'd been at the time, she had sensed the enormity of that fish's impression in stone. She'd held a piece of ancient history in her small hands.

Before trying to get some sleep, the women discussed the procedure for the swim. Sydney insisted on being the first through, which seemed the most logical choice considering her competence as a swimmer, Nicole's injury, and the fact that Danielle would have to be the last one out. Nicole turned on one of the lights. The group held one end of the webbing, while Sydney let it run through her hands as she paced off 30 feet. She tied the end of the webbing into her harness. This was about how long Danielle had decided the siphon was.

"But what if the siphon goes farther? Ya'll don't really know how far it is to the other side," Lynne said.

"You're right," Sydney said, tying a knot at the 30 foot point from her harness. "That's going to be the tough part for me. I'm going to have to have enough air left in my lungs to make it back if I can't get through. Going in will be easy since it'll be with the current, but coming back would be tough against that current. We'll have to work out some signals so you'll know if I need you to haul me out." Sydney's face was pale and serious as she contemplated the length of webbing laid out before them. "I'd better practice holding my breath a few times first to see what my limits are."

"Good idea," Nicole said. "When it's time for the real dive, you'll need to hyperventilate before you go in, to fill your lungs with as much oxygen as you can."

"Right. Let's try this a few times. Here, hold this at the knot." Sydney did some hearty exhaling and inhaling before holding her breath, walking away from them to simulate movement through the siphon. She made it to the end of the thirty feet and turned around to walk back. They watched her eyes water as she began letting little tiny breaths of air expel through her pursed lips. With three feet left to go, she had to take a big gulp of air.

"See?" Gabby said. "If Sydney can't do it, I know I'm not going to be able to."

"Just wait. Let me try it again. I think I can do it, and this time if I yank twice on the rope, pull me back toward you."

Again she drew in a deep breath and began walking out her length of the webbing. She stopped a moment, then turned around and came back toward them. At three feet from them she tugged twice and the group pulled the rope so hard she lunged toward them, almost falling on her face to the cave floor. "Hey! Not so hard, I'm not in the water yet." Their laughter loosened their dark mood and they tried it again. This time she made it back on her own.

Nicole frowned. "Once you get to the end of 30 feet, you should be on the other side where you can breathe. If we don't get the signal to pull you back, then we expect the three tugs that tell us you made it. That way we can let out enough slack for you to untie yourself. Don't take any chances if you're not through at 30 feet. No matter how close it looks. Promise?"

Sydney hesitated, then nodded her head, turning to hand Gabby the other end of the webbing. "When I get through, I'll give you the signal. Gabby, don't look so worried. It's going to be okay. I'm going to do this, and you will too. Remember, by the time it's your turn you'll know it can be done."

Gabby let out a sigh, "Well, I don't know. I really can't swim. And I'm not much good at holding my breath either. Watch. One, two, three . . ." and she took a giant breath, puffing her cheeks out like a frog.

They all burst out laughing and it was the threat of having to turn the light off that finally got everyone focused again on their test runs. Danielle and Nicole had each person try it at least once to get them ready.

"Remember the signals," Danielle said. "Two hard tugs means to haul Sydney back. Three hard tugs means she made it through."

"Hey, we have a total of 90 feet of webbing, remember?" Gabby said. "We used it at the cliff by the waterfall. Why couldn't Sydney just pull each person through? There'd be enough webbing for you to pull it back to you each time."

"Well, maybe we could use that in case of an emergency," Danielle said. "But we don't know how rough or twisted the walls in the siphon are, plus, the current is moving like a freight train through there already. You might ram into something or get hurt from going too fast. How about if we make four hard tugs to Sydney's end a signal for her to pull, just in case you get in a situation where you need it?"

Everyone agreed to the plan and Kate coached them on their codes. "Three tugs?"

"She got through."

"Two tugs?"

"Pull her back."

"Four tugs?"

"Sydney has to pull someone through from the other side."

"Five tugs?"

There was a confused pause and then Gabby blurted out, "Forget the siphon, let's take the elevator."

"Yeah," everyone groaned.

"Does anybody want to guess what time it is?" Melissa said as she pulled her logbook out for another entry.

"Time to get out of here," was the chorus.

"Besides that?" Melissa waited for an answer, tapping her foot.

No one had the energy to answer. It felt like an eternal moonless night to all of them.

"It's 11:15 on Sunday night. We'll be out of here tomorrow morning. Sweet dreams." Melissa hummed a soft tune as she prepared her sleeping spot.

"Mom? My ears hurt," Kate whimpered.

"Oh Kate, that's all we need right now. When did they start hurting?" Danielle tried to keep impatience out of her voice. She tucked a space blanket around Kate's small shoulders and smoothed some stringy bangs out of Kate's eyes.

"Just a little while ago, when we were practicing." Kate swallowed and held back tears.

"Well, maybe that's just from holding your breath. Try to think about other things. We'll be getting out of here soon and if they still hurt we'll take you to the doctor. Okay, honey?" Danielle patted Kate and kissed her cheek.

"I guess so, but . . ."

"Kate, just try and get some rest. I love you." Danielle turned to prepare her own bed.

Kate sniffled, then was silent.

Lynne and Melissa gave Nicole some more ibuprofen and another dose of antibiotics, making sure her dressings were snug. They made her as comfortable as possible and were relieved that she wasn't running a fever or feeling chilled. Turning out the light, they snuggled as close to each other as they could get, and tried to conserve what strength they had left.

Danielle was tired of thinking, planning, and trying to be organized. As she tried to relax, her whole body gave one of those muscle spasms, like a wooden puppet whose arms and legs fly out when you pull the string at the bottom. She tried again to relax and stifled a half-giggle, half-grimace at her body odor which came wafting up from within her coveralls; forty-eight hours of exertion in the mud and the dirt produced genuine sweat—no ladylike perspiration here.

In . . . out . . . breath in . . . breath out . . .

Gradually, as if coming in from a distance, something began pricking her consciousness. Her eardrums were signaling her brain of increasing pressure, as though they were climbing a mountain or diving into a deep ocean. Maybe it was just her sinuses. She tried to shrug it off, but her whole body was tingling with a dreadful expectancy. What in the world?

She was standing, turning on her light to face the stream with horror and understanding. Flash flood! She heard and felt it coming as she screamed to her team "Get high!" A solid wall of water crashed into their camp. In the back of her stunned mind she knew that summer storms outside must have sent a flash flood into the cave. Their only hope would be to try to get back up into the breakdown, but it had caught them completely off guard. The deluge was thundering upon them. Most of the women, groggy from sleep and lying wrapped up in their space blankets, instinctively flattened themselves to the ground and ducked their heads to avoid being thrown against the cave walls by the torrent. Women and supplies disappeared in the maelstrom. In that horrendous moment Danielle saw them disappear below the water at the same time she saw Kate turn around and reach for her hand.

"Kate!" Kate's thin fingertips slipped from Danielle's grasp as everything disappeared into a black well of nothingness.

11

Storming the Dragons Den

On the surface, the thunderstorm stomped down on them like a wet noisy beast. A deafening growl of thunder shook the ground and drowned out the person on the other end of the line as Max tried again to reach one of the dynamite experts. "Hello? Hello? I'm sorry to be calling at this hour, but this is an emergency. Is this Mrs. Thompson?" He plugged a finger into his other ear and strained to listen.

"Oh my Lord, has Ashby been in an accident?"

"No ma'am, he hasn't. I'm trying to reach him. This is Max Stewart with the Big Lick Grotto and Triangle Cave Rescue, I need to get hold of him as soon as possible." Max pulled his hood up over his head, his hair already dripping from the rain.

"Ashby left more than an hour ago," informed his wife, "Some of our neighbors down the road are having trouble getting their cows moved up to higher ground. The creek's rising here and . . ."

This was just the news Max didn't want to hear, and it was doubly grave: Ashby was not readily available, and the rains were causing the creeks to overflow their banks. "Can you call him, get a message to him? We have a cave rescue going on here at Dragons Den and we need him, now. People's lives are at stake."

"Well, I'll try but . . ."

"There are seven women trapped in this cave, Mrs. Thompson. These rains will flood the cave too. We'd appreciate anything you can do to get word to him."

"Just call me Sam, short for Samantha. Did you say women?"

"Yes. My wife and daughter are in there, so you see . . ."

"Mercy me, I'll call over there right away. And if I can't get him on the phone, I'll drive over," she said. "I'm sure Ashby will want to do everything he can to help."

Max gave her the number of the command post phone and dialed again, "Mariah, it's Max. Did I wake you?"

"Are you kidding? I've been on the phone most of the night. There's no way I can sleep until everyone's out of that cave," Mariah said. Mariah was an invaluable contact when it came to rescues; she was an NSS member, the Secretary of the Grotto and a long-time caver herself, as well as a family friend. "Have you made contact with them at all?"

"No, we haven't gotten to them yet, and we've got serious problems. The women are in the lower level, and the drop site is covered with new breakdown. This rain is the last thing we needed right now. Did you get any word from the hospital on the guy they pulled out?"

"He's in critical condition from hypothermia and his leg injuries, plus the shock. From what I hear, his buddies are the ones that should be in the hospital."

"Off the record, I'm tempted to agree with you. But we don't have time to play judge and jury now. It's raining like hell and the creek is rising. We need to get those women out fast!"

"What about Ashby, is he coming?"

"His wife's trying to reach him right now. But we need some cave divers. Can you call some and send them out? What's the weather report?"

"There's a flash flood warning in effect for the next hour or so. Then the storm's supposed to move off to the Northeast at a pretty good clip, so the rains should taper off soon."

"I'll leave someone here by the phone while I go fill Ernie in on what we've got so far. Make it quick, Mariah. I need to get some divers in to push that siphon from the resurgence."

"You can count on me. Max?"

118

"Yes?"

"Everything's going to be all right. You couldn't have a better IC than Ernie. And with you and the rest tackling the cave from every angle, you'll get them out. Danielle has a good head on her shoulders, and Nicole's a PA as well as an experienced caver. Kate can be mighty tough under pressure too. And isn't that Sydney a caver from TAG? You hang in there. And listen, my old man should be there any minute to give you a hand."

Max's boots created a wake through the rain and mud as he returned to the phone after briefing Ernie on the status of Operations. Mariah had called back within minutes to say some divers were on their way from West Virginia and would be there in maybe three hours.

"How's it going?" Mariah's husband sloshed up with a thermos of black coffee. They climbed into the car out of the storm. Hodag was tall and rangy; his rubber-like body was made for wriggling through tight passages and stretching across chasms. Petite Mariah, envious of his reach, had nicknamed him "Hodag," after a mythical cave beast.

"What do you have so far?"

"Ashby Thompson's wife is trying to reach him and have him come see if we can dynamite our way in. It's going to take that or heavy drills and tools to enlarge the waterfall passage or get through the breakdown over the drop."

Max and Hodag listened to the rain pelt the roof of the car and watched the lights of the other cavers weave through the omnipresent reporters.

"So who's in the cave with Danielle and Kate and Nicole?" Hodag said. "Isn't Sydney with 'em?"

"Yes. Along with three novices, Gabby, Melissa, and Lynne. A couple of them have kids and husbands."

"I know, I ran into a couple of the guys waiting in the tent with the Information Officer. They're pretty upset."

"Can you blame them? But it's not the women's fault. This was all caused by some . . . I can't even think of a name bad enough to call those guys. From what this guy, Tim, told me when we found him, they pulled the ropes up as a joke."

"A joke? God, can you believe some people?"

119

"He claims they were going to come back and lower the ropes before anyone got hurt. But apparently when the other two guys started climbing around above the drop, the whole thing came falling down. Some joke. Well the joke's got Tim in the hospital, and innocent people are paying the price. God help the other two if and when I get hold of 'em. That's for later. Right now we need to find a way to get the women out." Max glanced at Hodag and then stared out at the storm. They could hear the creek madly rushing by them, rising with every minute.

Hodag pulled the map of Dragons Den off the dashboard. "Do you think they'll try to swim out the siphon?"

Max paused for a moment, looking down at the gold wedding ring on his finger. It was worn and scratched from climbing and using his hands in every way imaginable, but he never took it off. Danielle's gold band, which was so small it could fit through Max's ring with room to spare, was just as covered with nicks; it was hardly even round anymore. When Max offered to buy her a diamond she said she'd rather have a simple gold band that she could wear everywhere, rather than some expensive bauble she'd have to leave at home.

"I have a feeling they will," Max said. "Danielle can't stand to sit around and do nothing. They'll have seen that the entrance to the drop is covered up. And I think she knows that no one can fit through the waterfall passage. We've speculated before about whether the siphon is passable. On the survey maps it looks to be about 30 feet through the siphon. A lot would depend on everyone's physical condition, and if they make it down the cliff and through the mazey breakdown area." Max shook his head slowly.

Hodag poured Max another cup of steaming coffee from his thermos. "So that's the bottom line."

"Did you say line?" Max said, turning quickly toward Hodag.

"Yeah, why?"

"You just gave me an idea. Why don't we put some supplies and a note in a watertight bag and send 'em down the waterfall on a line. Maybe, just maybe, they'll see it and that way they'll know what's going on and we'll know they're okay when they grab the bait. Come on, let's go."

Reining himself in, Max realized he'd need to send someone else to the cave, since he was still Chief of Operations and Planning. He started to ask Hodag, but Hodag was already making moves to gear up.

"I'm on my way. I'll grab another caver and we'll put something together to drop in there."

"Be sure and use strong line. We don't want the care package breaking off before they can get to it. And tie some of those blinking cave beacons on it. That ought to get their attention."

"Anything special you want to say to Danielle in the note?"

Max hesitated. "How 'bout 'Knock Three Times on the Ceiling if You Want Me?'"

Hodag gave him a thumb's up and headed for the cave, leaving Max to wait for the divers. Max knew he should rest, but it was difficult.

He couldn't stop thinking of the cave as his foe: a mountainous, hungry, stubborn dragon holding his Lady hostage. He'd gladly trade his life for hers. But this dragon was devious. It had taken others hostage as well. Kate. Danielle. The other women. Cavers and rescuers too.

Max came awake with a start. The rain had stopped and the first light of day was forcing its way through the clouds. The wind that had brought the rain into the valley was now chasing the clouds away, leaving a freshly washed sky where the rising sun was painting its morning colors. Max held his breath as he watched the golden light appear from behind the mountain, making the wet forest around him glisten and shine. Danielle was always seeing signs in things. He tried to see this as a sign that he had nothing to fear.

He was startled out of his trance by Tucker tapping at the window. "What's up?" he said, getting out of the car and pulling on his coveralls. He noticed two guys in cave garb behind Tucker. "Any news?"

"Well, no. Not about the women. But we have another problem. Ernie assigned me to serve as Security Officer and it looks like we've got us a situation." Tucker turned and pulled the two men from behind him, placing them in front of Max. They looked like any of the other cavers that had shown up to help with the rescue, at least as far as their gear went. But neither one would look Max in the eye.

"Who are you?"

The shorter of the two men shifted his weight and folded his arms across his chest. "I'm a reporter and he's the photographer for the "Blue Ridge Chronicle," we were just . . ."

"Weren't you asked for identification at the entrance to the cave? Didn't Entrance Control log you in?"

"We told her we were from the Pennsylvania Grotto."

There was nothing Max hated more than lies. "I'll have you arrested."

The men stood there stubbornly and shrugged as Max motioned them to move to the car.

"You put every caver in there at risk, including the people that are trapped below."

"Your wife and daughter are in there, right?" The reporter took out a pen and flipped through a dirty spiral-bound notepad.

Before Max could respond, Tucker said, "There's more. They were climbing around on the boulders near the breakdown, trying to see if they could get some pictures." Tucker shot a dark look at them and then back at Max, "And they knocked some more stuff loose. It's a miracle they didn't get crushed themselves."

"It's not a miracle," Max said low enough for only Tucker to hear, "it's a damn shame."

The reporter flipped his pad to a clean page and stepped up cockily, "You can't keep us out of that cave, it's your wife and kid you should have kept out. The public has a right to know what happened."

Tucker reached toward the reporter, who backed up and tripped over his gear bag to fall with a grunt into a large mud puddle. The cameraman lunged toward Tucker. Tucker swung, but Max caught his arm and stopped the cameraman with his shoulder. The photographer glared at Tucker, but with Max now between them, gave up the fight and instead turned around to help the reporter to his feet.

"Sorry," Tucker said. "I let him get to me. That was good, Max, I heard you had a black belt, but . . ."

"Yeah, I've got a black belt," Max said, "I use it to hold my

pants up. Here comes Ernie. He's not going to be happy about this."

"The Sheriff's already on his way," Max said as Ernie came within earshot. "We'll let him decide what to do with these two cowboys."

"All right," Ernie said. "Let's get on with the rescue. The dynamiter is here waiting on his marching orders."

They sent Ashby in with three cavers to survey the waterfall area and the breakdown area over the drop. Ashby was a dynamiting artist and had a sixth sense about the stability of caves as far as explosives went. He was known for setting his charges so accurately that he was kidded as being the creator of such geologic wonders as Natural Bridge and Chimney Rock. "Naw, them're the work of the good Lord Himself," he said. "But did you ever hear tell of Mount Rushmore?"

Feeling somewhat encouraged now that Ashby was inside, Max and Tucker entered the tent to brief the Resurgence Team. Although it was only 7:00 a.m., the sun was already heating up the tent. They rolled the tent sides up since the rain had stopped.

Max nodded his approval at the men and women waiting for their assignments. During his years of involvement with cave rescues, he never ceased to be amazed at the enthusiasm and energy of those who volunteered their time and energy. Exercises, mock rescues, classes and practice sessions honed their skills, resulting in dedicated, skilled, and tireless teams. The training and drills enabled them to stay in control and perform their functions despite the urgency and potential panic that surrounded any real rescue.

"I want to personally thank each one of you for coming," Max said. "For those of you who've just arrived, here's the situation. We have seven people trapped in the lower level of Dragons Den. The drop was covered when three men caused a massive breakdown. One has already been extricated from the cave and is in critical condition. The other two apparently left the cave." Max cleared his throat and looked away for a moment. "We can't get to the patients—six women and a young girl—through that original drop. It's much too unstable. There's a waterfall into the lower level but at the present time the passage to it's too narrow for

125

anyone to fit through. Ashby Thompson is seeing if he can blast it open, without endangering the women below."

"Do we know if the women are all right?" someone asked.

"We have to believe they are. Four of them are experienced cavers, and the other three are novices. Danielle, one of the leaders, knows that it might be possible to work through the cave to a siphon. I think they may try to come out that way, so that's where we'll concentrate our other efforts, with divers at the resurgence."

"How long have they been in there?" one of the rescuers said.

"We think the breakdown occurred sometime Saturday evening. They should have about 24-hours' worth of supplies in their packs, but it's now Monday morning so they're probably running out of food and batteries. The biggest concern right now is flash flooding. The rains have stopped, but the people in the cave are still in danger. You saw what the storm did to the creeks and roads. All that water is now working its way through the cave, which is bad news if the women are at or near the siphon. It's also going to present quite a problem for the divers since the current is strong even when there hasn't been any rain. But they'll give it their best shot."

Max glanced at his watch and pointed to various rescuers, assigning them to teams. "I don't have to tell you that these seven women are counting on us. Each one of them has families, children, friends, loved ones, waiting anxiously for their safe return."

As the teams moved to leave, Max said, "One more thing. Move fast but safe. Don't endanger yourself or your teammates. We have a big enough rescue without having to rescue one of you. Now let's do it!"

12

Turmoil

"Kate? Kate! NO!" Danielle screamed, waking the others into a mad scramble of confusion and panic. Flashlights clicked on and frightened faces leapt into view, eerie shadows dancing around them. Echoes of the scream bounced off the stone walls.

"I'm here, Mom, I'm here," Kate said, leaning over Danielle and placing a small hand firmly on each cheek. "Wake up. Please, mom. Look at me. It's all right, please don't cry." Kate heaved a sigh as Danielle's eyes locked into hers with recognition.

"Oh my God, Kate, I thought I'd lost you." Danielle embraced her daughter. "I'm okay, you guys. Turn off those lights." Looking around at them, she acquiesced. "Well, you can leave one of them on." She sat up, trying to stop trembling. "I'm sorry. I had a nightmare, but it seemed so real. Too real. I dreamt . . ." Danielle stopped in mid-sentence. Look out! Look out! Her intuition commanded her to action. "Grab your stuff," she said. "We're moving out of here. Move. Now! Quick!" She scrambled to her feet in a panic, gathering packs together.

"What?" Lynne said, pick up her gear and looking at the others.

"Why?" Gabby asked. "What's wrong now?"

"No time to explain, we have to move fast. Melissa, take us

back up through the breakdown. We have to get out of here."
Danielle grabbed her supplies and Kate's too. She pushed Kate
upward, spurring the team to action.

Sydney's eyes were bright with sudden comprehension as she
turned her back to the siphon and began helping the others. Before
they scrambled into the labyrinth, she looked around again to see
water backing up at an alarming rate. Water was pouring into the
siphon, bottlenecking in the very room where they'd decided to
bivouac. If they moved carefully and quickly they should be able to
reach the higher level. But they had to stay calm; it wouldn't do to
avoid drowning only to end up buried alive. She forced herself to
concentrate on each move, each twist, each physical effort through
the jumble.

Reminding each other to move gingerly, they worked their
way back up through the labyrinth, weaving through the nasty stuff
with intense determination. Danielle kept an especially close watch
on Nicole who battled pain with every motion. She couldn't
believe they were having to fight their way through the dangerous
maze again. What made it worse was knowing they would have to
retrace their moves a third time if they still planned to swim the
siphon.

They arrived, exhausted, on the other side.

"The water sounds so loud," Gabby said. Are you sure it won't
come up this far? How far is the waterfall past here, anyway? I
think I can hear it."

"It's raining outside, isn't it, Danielle?" Sydney said.
"Summer storm. And the water's backing up at the siphon. We
would have drowned if we had stayed there."

"Sweet Jesus," Gabby said. The water seemed determined to
do her in, one way or another. "I can't take this anymore. What
next?"

"How did you know? Was it your dream?" Sydney looked at
Danielle before she crouched near Nicole to check her bandages.
Unless Nicole started showing signs of fever, it was best not to
disturb them to check the wound underneath.

"It was Kate's ears, wasn't it?" Nicole said. "She was
complaining about her ears hurting. The incoming water increased
the air pressure and Kate's sensitive ears felt the change."

"I guess it was the combination of that and my dream. Maybe our Guardian Angel really is looking out for us," Danielle said. Her whole body felt like someone had picked her up by the ankles like a baseball bat and swung her against a brick wall. She couldn't remember ever feeling pretty or feminine. Had she ever worn silk or dainty sandals? Had she ever tossed her head saucily, making her silver earrings dance at Max as they toasted each other over a candlelight dinner?

Gabby shook her arm and demanded, "Now what? How do you know the water won't come up this far? Oh God, I don't want to drown." She released her grip on Danielle and began throwing her arms up and down in frustration; half as shrugs of helplessness and half as though in an effort to take flight and wing her way upward and out of there.

"Gabby, look at the walls of the cave," Danielle said. "There isn't any mud on them. If it had ever flooded this high, there would be mud banks and deposits left on the walls by the water. We're so much higher than the siphon now that it would take the Biblical flood to reach us. It's just a summer storm and once it passes, the water will drop back down, long before it will ever come up this far."

Gabby was not to be consoled. The cave seemed to close in suffocatingly around her. "What are we going to do? Isn't there some other way out of here? Some way that we won't drown or get crushed to death? Let's go back to where we were at first, to the bottom of the drop and just wait for them to come and get us."

"Are you forgetting what we had to go through to get here? It's still a bit of a hike back to the cliff, and we'd never make it up that thing anyway," Nicole said, pointing to her injured arm for emphasis. "Even if I had the use of both hands, I don't think I could climb it; not only is it straight up but it's wet. And which one of us could possibly lead it since we brought the webbing down with us? It would be suicide. Sheer suicide. And even if, by some miracle, we did make it up that cliff and to the drop area, I sure don't want to be beneath where they might be blasting, do you?"

"I don't know," Gabby said. All I know is that I'm tired and cold and hungry and I want to go home."

"Talk about being stuck between a rock and a hard place,"

129

Lynne said. "I feel like the earring I dropped down the bathroom sink—stuck in the pipes somewhere."

"Yeah, somebody call a plumber," Sydney chuckled weakly. But nobody was in the mood for jokes.

Danielle knelt down, hands palm up in supplication. "I'm sorry. I'm really sorry." They stared in silence as she bent her head to her hands, her shoulders shaking with dry heaves. The fabric of the team was disintegrating and she was almost ready to surrender.

Nicole rested her uninjured hand on Danielle's back and patted it a few times. "Look, none of this is your fault. The 'plumbers' are up there working on this. I'm sure they're doing all they can to get us out. You didn't cause this breakdown or my fall or the flood or any of that, you know."

"I know," Danielle said. "But maybe Gabby and Lynne are right."

"Stop beating yourself up," Sydney said. "We all made the decision to move on, and I still think it was the right one. And even though the plumbers are up there, it will take them a long time. We have to try. I'm sure this storm will pass and we can still swim the siphon."

"No way!" Gabby said. "Especially not now. You'll never get me in that water. I'm going to wait right here and they can just come and get me. We never should have tried to get out of here on our own in the first place. And I never should have come on this crazy trip."

Danielle looked at Nicole and they both knew it would do no good to try to argue with Gabby.

"Scoot on over here, Gabby; sit by me and help me get warm," Lynne said gently.

They tucked their hypothermia blankets tightly around themselves and turned their backs on the rest. Melissa approached Danielle and Nicole.

"I'll keep those two company while you figure something out. I'll do whatever you need me to do. And I still think we can get through the siphon. Or if you need me to, I'll stay with Gabby and you can all swim out to get help."

"Well one thing is for sure," Nicole said, "we need to stick together. But thank you for your offer. We'll do some discussing and then we'll all talk about what we should do. See if you can't get Gabby and Lynne to chill out."

Sydney and Kate joined Danielle and Nicole in an inventory of what they had left. Enough light for maybe eight hours, one last hot drink and one powerbar apiece.

"I still think swimming the siphon is our only chance," Sydney said. "It will be harder than ever for a diver to swim against that current after the rain they've had out there; but, hey! at least the current's on our side. We all agree we can't go back, right?"

The other three agreed. "There's no way I could make it back up that cliff," Nicole said. "And there's no way we're going to leave Gabby and Melissa here either. We're running out of time." She didn't want to tell them how much her arm hurt; she hated to admit that to herself.

"And out of food," Kate said, her eyes looking bigger than ever.

"And batteries," Sydney said.

"Okay, how about this," Danielle said. "We regroup, warm each other up as much as we can. Physically and mentally. Psych ourselves up to the max. Save as much of our lights as we can for tomorrow. And if the St. Bernard's haven't arrived with their flasks of hot brandy by tomorrow morning, we'll swim that siphon and get the heck out of here. Is it a plan?"

"It's fine with me if we can convince the rest of the group," Sydney said. I think we'd better warm 'em up before we present our proposal, don't you?" Sydney took her gloves off and wiped a smear of dirt from her forehead.

Nicole rifled through her bag and pulled out some stubby white candles. "Well, I don't have any marshmallows but we can toast some buns," she grinned.

"What do you mean, Nicole?" Kate was fairly drooling at the thought of how a fluffy, sweet white marshmallow would taste right now.

Sydney answered, smiling, "You can burn a candle underneath your hypothermia blanket, being careful not to touch the flame to it of course, and the warmth of the candle will heat you right up."

"Can I do it? Please? I'm really cold," Kate said.

"Of course. We'll each take a turn getting toasty and then

snuggle all up like bugs in a rug. We'll pretend we're sitting around a campfire and having a grand ol' time." Sydney touched Kate's muddy cheek with a fingertip and handed her a candle.

"I wish we really did have some marshmallows and graham crackers and Hershey bars," Kate said. "We could make s'mores. Can we tell some more stories?"

"Sure kid," Nicole said. She needed the distraction. The pain from her arm was barely responding to the Ibuprofen.

"Ghost stories?" Kate said, and shivered a little.

"I don't think so," Danielle said. She forced a smile as she found her place amongst the women. Another whole day to try to keep things positive and keep her own hopes high. She'd been so focused on the vision of them being out today that the thought of having to make it through yet another endless night was overwhelming. She was so tired of being responsible for everyone.

"Danielle?" Nicole, as if reading Danielle's mind, leaned over and gently put a hand on her padded knee. "We're going to make it. You're doing a good job. We're all doing a good job. Don't give up now."

Danielle smiled through tears but didn't trust herself to answer. She just nodded and put her hand on top of Nicole's.

They sat on the floor and arranged themselves as best they could to generate warmth beneath the hypothermia blankets. This was their third night in the depths of Dragons Den and although they had their camping system down to a routine, their emotions were balking at the effort. Dirty, hungry, tired, and anxious, they fought their inner battles—hope against despair. They told stories and talked of what wonderful things they would do when they got out, but the blackness around them bore down and their conversation dwindled to sighs and muffled whimpers. They gave up and drifted into restless sleep.

Even the cave seemed to sleep through the conspiratorial whispers between Gabby and Lynne. Furtively, the two of them gathered their personal packs and crept away from the group, making their way up toward the cliff.

"Are you sure this is the way?" Lynne glanced back toward the group. The sleeping women looked like a giant five-headed creature, its breath rising and falling under a dirty silver skin.

"Positive. See, here's another one of the marking tapes we left behind on the way in. And listen, the waterfall is sounding closer." Gabby picked her way along the cave floor. "Is that your last set of batteries? Your light's pretty dim." Gabby pulled Lynne closer to her side as they made their way down the passage. "Are you sure you want to do this with me?"

"Yeah, I guess. I'm not going to let you go alone." Lynne smacked her battery pack, trying to jolt more power out of her rapidly failing headlamp. "You think the rescuers will be able to hear us from the top of the waterfall? It's awfully loud and we'll be a hundred feet below it."

"They'll have to hear us. Anything to keep from swimming that siphon. Hey, your light's shot. Just walk right behind me; we'll have to share mine." Gabby shivered. She was glad Lynne had come with her. Lynne seemed as desperate to get home to her kids as she was. They wound through the passage and tried to keep a chatter going; conversation seemed to keep their fear at least at arm's length.

"The cliff shouldn't be much farther. What do you think Danielle and the rest are going to do when they find out we're gone?" Lynne was keeping one hand on Gabby from behind to keep from stumbling. Suddenly, they were engulfed in utter darkness.

"Shit! My light's out. I knew I should have brought along one of theirs." Gabby slumped toward Lynne and pulled her down to the dirt.

"We don't have any choice but to sit here and wait for them to come find us. Damn! What are we going to tell Danielle? And now we've used up two lights, too."

"I'll say it," Lynne said. "Shit!" Lynne gave a sad helpless laugh. "Shit, shit, shit, shit, shit. Shit!"

"We probably ought to eat something. I'm shaking," Lynne said. "I've only got one powerbar left. How much food do you have?"

"Well, you caught me. I have a chocolate bar stashed away that I was saving for a special occasion." Gabby fumbled with the buckles on her pack and groaned at the sound of its contents clattering to the ground.

Lynne leaned over to help feel around for the wayward articles when Gabby wailed, "My camera, I can't find my camera."

Removing their gloves, they lightly swept the dirt floor in semi-circles where they'd been huddled. "Got it."

The two of them huddled together, sucking on tiny bites of chocolate.

"So, how did you get to be a photographer anyway?" Lynne asked.

"I guess it's my way of capturing memories. I don't draw or paint or write songs, but I see lots of incredible things that I want to remember. I love to travel. I've got the wanderlust bad. Or good, depending on how you look at it. To me, it's good. To my husband, it's bad. Anyway. Pictures preserve things that will never happen again. And I can also express things that I wouldn't be able to describe to someone in words."

"I can't wait to see what these pictures will look like," Lynne said. "What do you think your husband will say?"

"I don't know. I don't even know if I'll show them to him, he's so unpredictable. All I can say is that he'll either love them or hate them. He'll just be thinking about how pissed he was that I was off on my own in the first place, and not appreciate the quality of the images. He's probably half glad that I'm in here and hoping I'll never return, since we argue so much; and half scared I won't come back. Weird, huh?" Gabby contemplated the discrepancy herself; it made even less sense to her down where there were no distractions. In her mind, you either loved someone or you didn't. She couldn't figure out how she got tangled up with someone that was so gray in that area. With her skills at focusing and producing sharp images, her view of him was awfully fuzzy. Or maybe her focus was fine and it was just that he kept moving around, changing his position.

"So why do you stay with him?" Lynne was thinking about Tim and her own choices.

"I ask myself that every day," Gabby sighed. "I guess the wanderlust in me, the part that believes there's something special to see around every corner, hasn't quit believing that maybe there's hope for us around the next bend. I keep thinking that one day I'll take just the right picture and hand it to him, and he'll look at it and really see who I am. Maybe that's why I like taking pictures of Andrew, our son. To prove that good can come out of us."

As Gabby spoke, she pictured her son's rusty blond hair and impish nose. She had a picture of him in hipwaders in their favorite mountain stream, holding up a citation brook trout. In the foreground, mirrored in a small pool of the stream, was her reflection, just faintly rippled by the underlying current, the camera hiding all her face except for her lips curved in a half smile.

"Hey, I'm sorry I got you into this mess." Gabby was close to tears.

"Well I wasn't about to let you go alone. Besides, it was my choice; it's not like you forced me or anything," Lynne said. "Danielle and the rest will find us. We just have to sit tight and wait. Do you think they could hear us if we hollered?"

"Please don't! They'll find us soon enough. And you know they're going to be really mad at us for leaving." Gabby pulled her knees to her chest and wrapped her arms around them, tucking herself into a protective ball. The two women leaned against each other, back to back, taking comfort in the mutual warmth and the sounds of their breathing. Then Gabby realized that Lynne was trembling. "Are you okay?"

"I guess," Lynne said, trying to keep her teeth from chattering. "Just a little cold."

"Look, spread your space blanket on the ground and we'll curl up next to each other with mine on top. A Gabby-Lynne sandwich. We've got to get you warm." Gabby rustled around in the blackness, helping Lynne with the blanket.

Lynne purred with relief. She patted Gabby's arm wrapped snugly around her waist like a seat belt. "Thanks."

"Any time."

They hugged each other close. "Listen, I think I hear them coming. At least it better be them and not some giant cave rat or something." They shrank against each other, not sure whether to get up and run to or from the clattering and scraping sounds heading in their direction. "It's Danielle. And Melissa."

Lynne stood up first, Gabby behind her. Gabby wanted to see what kind of expression was on Danielle's face before she said anything. But she was blinded by the glare of Danielle's headlamp;

Danielle's face was hidden in the shadows as Lynne and Gabby were cast in the spotlight. They couldn't help but feel like they were suddenly on trial.

"Don't say it," Gabby said.

"Say what?" Danielle said. Her voice, though cold, sounded on the verge of breaking.

"Anything. Just don't say anything. No lectures, please. I know we . . . I . . . screwed up. This was my idea. Lynne came along because she didn't want me to go alone." Gabby still couldn't see Danielle's face. She was grateful for the light, but at this particular moment almost wished she were back in the cloak of darkness.

Danielle was silent, carefully choosing her words. "Look. I'm just glad you're both all right. We've been frantic thinking you might have gotten lost or hurt or something." Danielle swallowed and turned her headlamp off as she clicked on her small flashlight for enough light to see each other. "And yes, I'm mad that you left the group. I guess I feel like a mother whose child runs away and then comes back home. She doesn't know whether to spank her or hug her." An angry tear streaked down her cheek and Danielle looked away to regain her composure. "Oh, what the heck," she sighed and grabbed Gabby and Lynne close. "I'm glad you're both okay."

"I'm sorry we went off like that, Danielle," Gabby said. "I just don't think I can swim that thing. I wanted to come back here and wait for the rescuers to reach us through the waterfall. You said they'd be trying to open it up, right?"

"But Gabby, it's not safe to be close to where they'll be blasting. Where do you think the rocks and pieces will go when they set off the dynamite? And we have no idea how long it will take them. It could be days. We don't have that much time. And how in the world did you think you were going to get back up that cliff?" Danielle's voice rose shrilly. "We all talked about what our plan would be and I thought we were all in agreement. We're in this together, aren't we?"

"I can't swim, Danielle, haven't you been listening? I can't swim. You can, so you don't know how I feel. I'll just wait here. Please? They'll break through eventually." Gabby stood stiffly,

136

refusing to budge. "We don't have time to wait for them. We have to try. We're not helpless, we can try to get out on our own," Melissa said.

"But the siphon's flooded! We can't swim it when the room above it is full of water," Gabby said, her chin jerking.

"Well, we've been checking out the creek level on the way up here and I truly believe it's receded. It must've stopped raining outside. We won't know for sure until we get back to that room. And of course we won't attempt it if it's still flooded. But we're almost out of light and food as it is now. It's really our best chance."

"Oh God," Gabby whispered.

"C'mon, Gabby," Lynne said, "We can do this. We'll show everyone we can save our own butts."

"Okay, okay. Let's go back with the rest of the gang before they start wondering if we've all gotten lost." Gabby squared her shoulders and collected her gear, making sure that her Minolta was safe and secure.

"That's the spirit," Danielle said. She patted Gabby on the back and they moved off down the passageway. The tension dissolved from their necks and shoulders, and tired smiles softened the shadows beneath their eyes.

KA-BOOM!

The explosion beyond and above them sent rocks and debris plummeting, back near the waterfall. Slivers of stone rained down into the room they'd been standing in just moments before. The blast was deafening and they could smell and even taste the acrid chemicals settling down from above.

"Holy cow!" Lynne said. "We're gonna die!" The color drained from her face, but she sucked in a deep breath and hollered, "Let's get out of here!"

Although the ground was uneven and rocky, they seemed to fly all the way back to the others. They collapsed in a pile amidst the cheers of Nicole, Sydney, and Kate. "You found them," Kate cried. "But what was that awful noise? Are they blasting?"

"Yes, they're blasting all right," Lynne said. "Ya'll heard it too? I'm not surprised. We felt it even though we hadn't even made it to the base of the cliff yet," Lynne panted. "Thank God

Melissa and Danielle found us when they did. We might have been history."

"I'm really sorry we left," Gabby said. "Maybe hunger is making me crazy."

"Well, we're glad you came back," Kate said, moving next to Gabby and squeezing her tightly around the waist. "We'd never leave without you."

13

Current Events

Ashby wiped his grimy face with an even grimier bandanna. His eardrums still resonated with the sound of the first charge.

"Always did like the '1812 Overture,'" he joked dryly to himself. "You kin come out now," he hollered to the cavers still crouched behind some boulders. He suppressed a chuckle at the wide eyes and open mouths of the young rescuers assigned to help him. "Haven't you ever heard dynamite before?" The trio shook their heads cautiously, as if afraid any sudden movements might bring the whole cave down. He'd made them pull up the line that held the care package so falling debris couldn't sever the rope or damage its contents, and then had them move a safe distance away when he detonated the charge. Anyone too close could get a concussion from the compressed air. Many a time a blast had blown out his carbide lamp.

"Let me check her out and see how we did," he said, hoping the matter-of-factness in his voice would put them at ease. He knew cavers didn't like anything rattling the rafters or disturbing the underground framework of any cave. Some places cavers wouldn't dare sneeze for fear of disturbing the balance of nature, but when there were lives at stake, he was as steady as a sculptor and as skillful as a surgeon. And he just loved grand openings.

Despite the fragility of some parts of this cave, other sections seemed built to last through eternity. Passages with massive walls of solid limestone were carved through the mountain and seemed impervious to dynamite. Ashby liked nothing better than to read between the cave's lines and discover its secrets. To find its Achilles' heel. That was the way to free its victims without destroying the beauty of the beast.

The waterfall quickly whisked away the dust and powder from the explosion. Ashby grunted as he pulled up his muddy pants' legs to crouch down and check the impact of the dynamite on the narrow passage. He had rejected the idea of dynamiting the breakdown pile. "One shot and the whole kit'n caboodle would be down on top of 'em." Or out from under us, he added silently.

Lord, my body's getting too old to do this, he thought. But his mind was as spry as a billy goat and his sixty years' of experience more than made up for being 76. Sometimes when yet another birthday rolled around, he'd reach down and ruffle the thick fur of his great cream-colored German Shepherd, Mack, pointing out that he was still a teenager—in dog years. Mack would promptly reply with a baritone bark, wagging his plume of a tail in agreement. Folks knew they could put stock in Mack's opinions; he'd survived a run-in with a bear up on Catawba Mountain and had the shoulder-to-shoulder scar to prove it. Ashby had Mack's tenacity, and was determined to face this opponent with just as much heart.

"Well, we made us a dent, but we've got a long ways to go," he informed his helpers. "We need to open her up like a New York subway. She's narrower and more stubborn than I thought. A prim'n proper virgin that's gonna take some patience and a bit of gentlemanly persuasion." He paused as he noticed one of the young cavers was blushing furiously. Ashby coughed and tried to redeem himself. "We don't have time for a long courtship. I just mean that to make the opening bigger will take lots of small blasts, rather than one big one." He felt like Michelangelo standing before a fresh slab of marble, chisel pointed, praying for divine guidance.

Ashby took the one-inch carbide steel star drill, and held it in place on just the right spot of the wall. He motioned to the blusher, a local high school boy named Kyle, to hold it in place. "You're gonna have to hold it steady, son. Like holding a football for the kicker. Hold it right there, don't move. Keep those safety glasses on and look away too, 'cause the chips will fly. Ready?"

He took another second to make sure everyone had helmets on. He picked up his hammer. As he raised it, Kyle took one hand off the drill.

"I'm not going to hit you," Ashby said, "long as you hold her steady. I've been doing this since you were knee-high to a grasshopper. Trust me. We can't get no electric drill back in here. We just have to do it by hand, bit by bit. Bit by bit, get it?"

Kyle nodded and braced firmly for Ashby's first stroke. The hammer made solid contact with the butt of the drill. After each strike, Kyle had to turn the star-shaped bit a half-turn for the next blow. A slow, tedious process, but it ate away at the rock, gouging out pieces to make a hole for the stick of dynamite.

Clang! Turn. Clang! Turn.

The rhythm was irresistible. Ashby's gravelly voice struck up,

"John Henry said to the Captain (CLANG!)

You can put your faith in this man (CLANG!)

Before I'll let this cave get me down (CLANG!)

I'll die with this hammer in my hand, Lord, Lord (CLANG!)

I'll die with this hammer in my hand." (CLANG!)

Ashby ignored the giggles of the other cavers. At least his caterwauling kept their minds off the risks of dynamiting.

Satisfied that the hole was the proper depth, he hooked the hammer on his belt and clapped Kyle on the back. "That oughta do 'er. Good job, son." He stuck a small rubber hose in the hole to blow out the debris. Flakes flew out, as if the cave-dragon was sneezing. Dust clung to Ashby's wiry gray hair, making him look like a mad scientist. He shone a flashlight into the hole and hummed a few more snatches of "John Henry."

He took a stick of dynamite out of his canvas bag and drilled a small hole in the end of it. From a separate padded case he lifted out a blasting cap. He attached wires to the cap and inserted it into the dynamite. Then he attached another set of wires to the ones on the blasting cap. The stick of dynamite slid snugly into the hole he'd drilled, with the wires running to a safe distance away.

As he assembled all the components, Ashby subconsciously slowed his breathing, even his heartbeat, aware of the power

143

potential of the chemicals in his hands. Sweat popped out on his wrinkled forehead. He never let himself become complacent about this work; complacency would breed carelessness, and send them all to Kingdom Come.

Satisfied that everything was properly prepared, he shooed his helpers back to a safe distance and crouched behind a solid wall. "Fire in the hole!" he shouted and detonated the charge. The explosion sounded like half a dozen M-80 firecrackers and once again, pieces of the wall gave way at the entrance of the tunnel. He kept his bandanna over his nose and breathed through his mouth to avoid the acrid odor of the powder.

No one moved until the dust settled and the only sound remaining was the steady noise of the waterfall. Ashby felt like a dentist drilling cavities and pulling teeth, complete with a sink of water for the patient to spit into. So far, so good.

The jangling of the field telephone startled them. "Just can't get used to a dang telly-phone in a cave," Ashby grumbled. "Answer that thing, Kyle, and see what they want."

"Dynamite Team here. This is Kyle." A curious look flickered across his face as he handed the phone to Ashby, "It's . . . it's your wife, sir."

"My wife? Samantha? Why, that woman don't give me a moment's peace." He took the phone, trying to act annoyed, but he was obviously pleased. "Samantha? What in the world are you doin' calling me in here? I'm smack dab in the middle of trying to bust some folks out of this cave and . . ." He paused obediently to listen and turned his back on the others so they wouldn't see him smiling.

"You be careful in there," his wife said.

"Now, we gotta get these women and that little girl out of this cave. And I have to stay here doin' everything I can until they're out."

"Just don't go doing anything crazy, Ashby. I know you and how indestructible you think you are. Just take care of yourself or I'll . . . I'll come in there myself and . . ." Samantha paused. "You just be safe, Ashby, and don't you worry about me. You go on and get those womenfolk out of there. You hear?"

"I knew you'd understand, Samantha. Hey, you'd better thank

that Ernie feller for letting you gab on his phone. You got my solemn oath I'll be careful. You ain't rid of me yet, Baby Doll. You go on home and I'll be home directly." Before handing the phone back to Kyle he added in a stage whisper, "You still got that red silk nightie I got you for your birthday?" He winked at Kyle and then bid Samantha good-bye.

"Nothing like some dynamite to make a man feel frisky," he chuckled.

The phone jangled again almost immediately. This time it was Ernie wanting to know how the blasting was progressing. "I'd have a tunnel blasted clear through to the other side of the mountain if it weren't for all the infernal phone calls," Ashby said, and hung up.

The phone range again immediately.

"Ernie," Ashby said, "I hate to say this, but it's probably going to take a day or two, maybe even three or four to get a passage big enough for someone to crawl through and drop to the lower level. If any of those other blasters get here, we can work in shifts around the clock and keep a steady push on her. It has to be lots of small charges to keep from caving everything in; on them and on us."

Ashby handed the phone to Kyle and turned back to his work.

"Ernie, this is Kyle. We could use some hot coffee and a couple of us are starting to drag a little. Can you send us two fresh recruits and a thermos full of high-test?" He gave a thumbs-up to the other cavers and paused as Ashby hollered something to him.

"And Ashby said to tell you some apple pie a la mode would sure be nice."

"We'll see what we can do, Kyle," Ernie said. "I'll get back with you and the team after I talk with Max. Keep us posted."

Ernie gave orders to take care of the Dynamite Team's requests (including orders to one of his go-fers to rustle up some apple pie, and pack it carefully in a small cooler), then sat down for a moment. He was under a great deal of pressure. He had to keep the momentum of the rescue at full speed. Experience had taught him that sometimes when rescuers can't see the patients, it's possible to lose sight of the urgency of the situation. He had to help them remember that lives depended on accomplishing their various tasks as quickly as possible. In contrast, on a mission where the rescuers can see and hear the suffering and fright of a patient, it's possible to become so concerned that the patient's feelings overwhelm their own caution and judgment. His job was to keep the whole operation focused and on track, with the right proportions of urgency and objectivity. Ernie ran his hand through his salt-and-pepper hair and cranked the handle of the phone that linked him to the resurgence.

"Max? What's the status of the Resurgence Team?"

"We're almost to the siphon now," Max said. "I've stationed two people to log everyone in and out of this end of the cave. There are three stretcher teams at the entrance ready for when we bring them out. Of course, I'm hoping no one will need a stretcher. There are four people with me running the phone line and lugging the communications gear. We've got a diver here, Charlie, with his six support personnel; and three EMT's. That makes a total of fifteen of us in the cave at this end."

Max unshouldered his pack as they reached another tight crawlway. The others started passing gear, bucket brigade style. A veritable army had descended into the cave, but if they had to carry out seven people, all the equipment and every hand was necessary.

"Once you get the team established," Ernie said over the phone, "you need to return to the surface to resume your duties as Operations and Planning Officer, Max . . . How's the water level at that end? It's totally cleared off up here."

"Looks like it's peaked out, but it's still high. At least it's not the raging river it was a few hours ago. We're going to push through this tight spot and get our diver in. We'll keep you posted. And I'll be up as soon as the team's in place."

Half an hour later, they finally reached the downstream end of the siphon. Murky water flowed from under the ceiling. Charlie, the diver, zipped up his wet-suit and put on his scuba tank. An extra tank and a waterproof bag of supplies were readied on a line for him to pull through once he reached the other side. Charlie prepared slowly and methodically. He checked and rechecked his regulator and added another weight to his belt as the wet-suit would tend to make him float.

When he was ready, he said, "Look at the current coming through there."

"I don't want you to put yourself in danger," Max said.

148

"If you think you can get through, at least give it your best shot."

The water from the siphon flowed out into a circular pool on the bank of which the team members stood. It bubbled and swirled around before making its way on out of the cave, looking for all the world like a giant, cold Jacuzzi.

The team watched as Charlie disappeared into its bubbles.

Within minutes, he was back. He grabbed outstretched hands and came out of the water. He raised his mask and ran a dripping hand over his face.

"Swam as hard as I could and stayed in one place." He pulled the mask back on and again submerged. He was gone longer this time.

"Well, I was able to tell one thing," Charlie said after surfacing. "It's going to be a tight fit with this tank on. And that current is bad news."

"You want to rest?" Max asked.

"It's okay, I'll try it one more time. It's got me mad now." Charlie readjusted his tank and inserted his mouthpiece. He went under again and was back almost at once.

"I'm sorry. The current's way too strong."

All they could do now was wait.

"Pickets," said Max, staring at the swirling water.

"What?" Charlie said, thinking perhaps Max had lost his mind. He pictured Max and the rest of them marching around the entrance of the cave waving posters and signs chanting, "Set the Women Free" and "Damn the Siphon." The others, too, looked at Max uncertainly.

"Pickets and stemples. Get Ernie on the phone. We need pickets and stemples."

"What are you talking about?" Charlie said.

"Pickets are short, metal poles, pointed at the bottom like the pickets of a fence. You can stab them into the mud floor of the siphon and pull yourself forward, like climbing a vertical peg-board in a gym. If the floor is rocky, you can screw in a stemple."

It would be hard work, but by the time the equipment arrived there ought to be more divers to assist Charlie. Once one of them made it all the way through to the other side, he could pull through

149

a nylon rope and remove the pickets and stemples. The divers could then pull themselves through on the rope.

"That will take a while," Ernie said, when the request had been made. "But another diver is on his way to give Charlie a hand if he needs it."

"Okay," Max said. "I'm on my way back. We'll leave Chris and Mark here at the siphon." Max took one last look at the siphon before heading out of the cave.

14

The Siphon

Sydney shucked her muddy coveralls. Her lithe, pale body glowed with a ghostly radiance in the light of Melissa's fluorescent cylume stick. Cave dirt had worked its way through her coveralls, through her polypro long-johns, and onto both cheeks of her lace-trimmed panties. She modestly tugged them up over her hip-bones sighing, "I know, I've got a buddy mutt." The pale blue shadows under her eyes intensified the glitter of her steel blue irises. "I can feel the sunshine calling to me from the other side. This is going to work, I just know it." She looked at her friends' faces for confirmation and bent over to lace her boots back on, sans socks. Then she straightened up to buckle her harness. She would use a carabiner on it to maintain control over her speed. Melissa gathered up Sydney's discarded cave clothes, rolled them up and wrapped them tightly in a plastic trash bag.

"This is it," Sydney said. "Pay attention to my signals. This webbing is my life-line, you know. Remember playing telephone with two tin cans and a piece of string?" She knew she was chattering but it helped keep her mind off the fear in the pit of her stomach.

"Here's your helmet, Sydney." Kate looked at Sydney's womanly figure with admiration and envy. She wondered what it would feel like to be a grown-up woman like Sydney. "I'll put your crystal necklace in my pack for you if you want. I'd hate to see you lose it."

"Thanks, Kate. You're always so thoughtful."

"You're welcome. I know we've already said a prayer and everything," Kate went on, "but I think Nicole ought to say one of her Latin things."

"How about *Forsan et haec olim meminisse juvabit*," Nicole said.

"Probably means 'you bit off more than you can chew,'" Gabby mumbled.

"No, it means, Perhaps this too will be a pleasure to look back on one day."

Gabby snorted and looked away,

"I'll bet I look pretty wild, don't I? Like an Amazon woman or something." Sydney squared her shoulders and rubbed her arms up and down with her hands. No time for dawdling, goosebumps were already showing on her exposed skin. Wordlessly, her six cave sisters surrounded her in a group hug. There were no tears, perhaps there were none left. Only a somber yearning to be on the other side, through that dark, submerged, unknown passage. "Does everyone remember the signals?"

The women recited: "Two tugs—pull you back, three tugs—you got through, four tugs—you pull from the other side."

Danielle was quick to add, "I've anchored the tail-end of the webbing to that boulder behind us. You've got thirty feet, Sydney. We'll be holding onto the line from the middle; that way we can feel your signals. We'll all help hold the line in case you need to be hauled back in. Lynne, why don't you get in front?"

Lynne sat down where she could brace her feet against a ledge and picked up the webbing, nodding to Sydney that she was ready. Her stomach was growling but she ignored it.

Sydney snugged up her helmet's chin strap, then started breathing deeply to prepare her lungs for the plunge. She closed her eyes, imagining blue skies and warm food. "The longer I wait, the harder this will be," she whispered, and then in a firm voice, "Got a bottle of champagne to smash on my hull? Let's launch this ship."

Hugging her clothes-parcel to her chest, she lowered herself

into the current. "Brrrr! Cold." If it hadn't been for the webbing, she would have immediately been sucked under the roof. She clung tightly to the nylon, forcing her feet downward until she felt them bouncing up and down off the bottom of the channel. "It's really strong," she yelled above the rushing stream. "Let's try this once to make sure you're going to be able to pull me out if you have to." She yanked on the webbing twice and with great effort the group dragged her in toward the edge. "Okay. Be sure you go feet first, and your helmet's snug. I'm going now. Be ready."

The water was pulling at her. She glanced up one last time at the women gathered on the bank, then yelled, "Here I go!"

Squeezing her eyes shut tight, she gulped one last breath, and felt the water take her, down . . . under . . . fast . . . sliding under the submerged ceiling.

Sydney's thoughts raced as she plummeted through the siphon, "It's so cold and black . . . What's that snaky thing slithering around my legs? Oh, the webbing. It's okay . . . I'm moving so fast . . . Can't let go . . . Got to stay in control . . . The current's so strong. Am I really doing this or will I wake up in my warm bed at home, glad it was just a dream? I'm so cold . . . ouch! That rock was sharp. Let out a little breath . . . Don't wonder how much longer it will be. Try not to think about breathing. Where's the other end? How long has it been? How far have I gone? What if the hole at the other end is too small? What if I'm pinned and drown? My hands are numb from holding this slippery webbing. I can't tell how fast it's sliding through my hands. How much longer. . . Could they pull me back if I signaled? How many feet do I have left?"

Her lungs screamed for air. Then she felt the current slacken. She instinctively shoved her feet down and thrust her body upward, leaping for the sky. Air! She drank it in with a deep gasp as she burst through the surface.

Chris and Mark dropped their hot drinks and rushed into the water. When they grabbed Sydney, she screamed, then relaxed as she realized who they were. Together they struggled out of the water and got Sydney wrapped in a blanket. The end of the webbing was still tied to her harness. Chris started to untie it, but Sydney stopped her.

"It's okay, it's okay. You made it! My name is Chris and I'm with the rescue team. Take your time, catch your breath. What's your name? Mark, get on the phone. Call IC. Tell them one of the women just came through the siphon. Get Max down here, right now." She tried to untie the knot again, but Sydney gestured her to wait.

"I have to pull it . . . three . . . three times," Sydney said. "I have to let them know . . . I made it. My name is Sydney. Sydney. And I made it!" She gave the lifeline three firm tugs, then untied it, sobbing with joy and relief.

"Sydney is out, and she's okay," Mark said over the phone.

"Are the rest of them okay?" Chris asked Sydney.

"Yes, they're going to swim through too. Nicole hurt her arm, but she'll be okay. There is one . . ." Sydney paused.

"One?" Chris asked.

"One person doesn't think she can swim the siphon. Her name's Gabby. She can't swim. Is there any other way you can get her out? We heard the dynamite back past the waterfall. How long would it take to get through that way?" Sydney gratefully accepted a cup of steaming coffee and smiled with pleasure as its warmth spread through her limbs.

"They have a dynamite team working on it, but from what we've heard, it could take them days to get through. There's a diver on his way here right now. We'll find a way to help everyone out, including your friend Gabby. Since we can use your webbing, and we know it's passable, I imagine we'll use the siphon, just like you did. Max and Ernie will have the final say." Chris handed her some more coffee. "So, how was the swim? Was it bad? How long and tight is the siphon?" Chris kept looking over her shoulder, anxious for Max and the rest to arrive. She offered a sandwich from the rescue supplies to Sydney who grabbed it hungrily.

"Bad? I'm not sure that's the word I'd use. I wouldn't want to do it again any time soon, but it did get me out of there, didn't it? I think Lynne is coming next. I wish there was some way to let her know what to expect, and that you're here."

"Well, they know you were successful from your signal, right?" Chris said. "And we'll give them all the support they need. I saw the webbing being pulled back through for the next person."

156

Back at the siphon, the women cried out with relief as Lynne felt Sydney's three tugs. "That's it, three! She made it, she made it! We're going to get out of here." Lynne pulled in the dripping webbing. "I'm tying in. Here, someone take the webbing for me. It's my turn!"

Danielle took hold of the line. "Thank God, I am so glad she got through. It didn't seem like it took that long, did it? Everyone, take just the bare minimum, just plan on leaving your packs here. The food's all gone and the batteries are too. Someone will just have to come back and get them another time."

"Not me," Lynne said.

"I know, I know. I didn't expect that it would be any of you retrieving the gear. We'll make other arrangements for that. That's the least of our worries right now. Let's just make sure we all get out of here in one piece."

Danielle was cautiously optimistic. One out, six to go. She caught a glimpse of Gabby who was sitting wordlessly with her back to the siphon. Maybe if Gabby sees a few of the others make it, she'll come around, Danielle hoped. Danielle hugged Kate and then braced herself to hold the webbing for Lynne.

"Ready or not, here I come," said Lynne. She stood poised at the edge, testing the waters with a pale toe.

"That's quite a bruise you've got there, Lynne. Did you get that here in the cave?" Nicole looked concerned; the bruise was yellowing, it wasn't recent.

"Yeah. Well, no, actually. It's one of the reasons why I came on this trip in the first place. Don't look so serious, ya'll. Here I am all pumped up and ready to do this daring dive and you're worried about a little ol' bruise. That's all in the past now. Lighten up. I'm ready to rock and roll."

"Hey girl, I like your red undies," Melissa teased.

Lynne did a flirty model pose. "Ya'll like these? Well, my momma always said to wear clean underwear in case you're in an accident."

Kate giggled and pointed to Lynne's muddy backside. "Uh, Lynne, they don't look too clean to me."

"You're right, Kate. Maybe I should go skinny-dipping. Just take them off and wear my birthday suit. Hey, this is like getting

157

born again, isn't it?" Lynne stuck her thumbs in the sides of the panties to strip them off but Danielle interrupted,

"You'd better quit messin' around and get in the water before we run out of light. Let's move it." Danielle was glad everyone was trying to be lighthearted about this life and death situation, but she had to wait until they were all safely on the other side before she could joke about anything.

"Okay, okay. See ya later, ladies." Lynne took several deep breaths, then let out a screech as she entered the water. Shoot, she'd like to see ol' Tim do something brave like this. He'd never make it. As scary as it was, she felt pretty calm inside.

"Here goes," she shouted and let the water take her. As the current carried her through, she flashed back to each of her three children's births. Laboring and pushing and expelling them into the world had taken every muscle in her body. This time she could let someone else do the work. "C'mon momma dragon, push. Push!" She gave herself up to the force of the rushing current. The faces of her children appeared and she exhilarated in the ride.

She surfaced on the other side like a breaching dolphin, choking a little as a splash caught her in the mouth.

"Lynne!" Sydney said. "You made it!"

Lights flashed around her, telling her that Sydney wasn't the only person on her welcoming committee. Lynne shook her helmeted head and squinted. Two rescuers were holding out their hands. As she reached for them, she realized she'd been stripped of her red panties by the powerful current. "Oh, what the heck," she said. She let the two cavers pull her up out of the water, untied the webbing, gave it three strong tugs and let it go.

Mark chivalrously turned his back and tended to the phone while Chris wrapped Lynne up in a dry blanket.

"Hey, it's cool," Lynne smiled at Mark, "It's okay to look, everyone looks. It's not okay to point or laugh though. And of course, applause is always appreciated." Lynne pulled the blanket more tightly around herself as her wet hair dripped down her shoulders. "I just want to thank you kind people for being here and pulling me out. That's what I call service. Now if you can help the rest of my friends make their debut, we can go get something to eat. I'm starving. Hey, you there with the telephone, how about ordering a pizza?" Lynne suddenly felt guilty for thinking of food while the rest of them still had the siphon to swim. She hoped it was be as easy for them as it had been for her. It was just that she felt so unbearably proud of herself she wanted to party till the cows came home.

Mark surprised her by asking, "Pepperoni or mushroom? And how about a sandwich and some hot coffee in the meantime?" He winked at her.

She winked back. "Make mine with everything, please. This woman's alive and kickin.'" She took her helmet off, and shook her tangled curls out with a saucy grin.

Her smile faded to puzzlement when Mark handed her the phone. "There's someone on the phone for you. The call was patched in from the hospital. Someone by the name of Tim." Mark and Chris exchanged worried looks, and held their tongues.

Lynne, still high on her death-defying feat, sat rigidly still when it registered who the caller was. "Tim? I don't want to talk to him. From the hospital? What's he doing in the hospital?"

Mark held the phone out to Lynne as though it were on fire. "Here, you talk to him, he says he wants to apologize."

"Apologize? What does he want to apologize for?"

Mark covered up the mouthpiece of the phone and said hesitantly, "He got hurt here in the cave. Apparently he and two other guys pulled up your ropes as a joke and . . ."

"What?" Lynne's eyes narrowed and her face flushed crimson. "Give me that phone." Her voice was like a knife, "Tim? What the hell did you do?"

She could barely hear him answer, "I'm sorry baby, I'm . . ."

Lynne's voice gusted with full fury and she didn't care that Mark and Chris and Sydney could hear every word. "This is it, Tim. I never want to see you again."

"But if you hadn't gone in the cave in the first place . . ."

She lowered the receiver to ask Mark, "What is it you say when you're finished? Never mind, I just remembered." She raised the phone back up to her mouth and said, "Over. Over and out." She handed the phone back to Mark, then turned to Sydney to help welcome the others.

Kate had no doubts about her dive as she peeled down to her

body suit. Her tummy was grumbling with hunger, but she was ready for her turn.

"Mom, don't look at me like that. I'm a good swimmer and I'll be fine. I can swim underwater the length of the pool at Day Camp, so this will be easy. The current will take me right through. Please don't cry. You know how Daddy always says not to give your fears to me. Well, he's right. I'm more worried about you guys; do you want me to come through last?"

"No, Kate. It's just that I love you and . . ." Danielle said. She knew Kate was right, there was nothing more to say. "Go for it, Sweetie. I love you. Remember that, no matter what happens."

Kate slipped into the water and felt right at home. She always loved to swim and actually enjoyed swimming under water more than doing the crawl or breast-stroke on the surface. This water was colder than the pool back at Day Camp, but it still had that silky, slippery feel that made her want to glide and undulate like an otter.

The elements didn't frighten her. Growing up on rope and underground had taught her to have confidence in herself, her team, and her equipment. What did frighten her were lies, apathy, nightmares. Grown-ups arguing for no apparent reason was far more disconcerting than standing at the edge of a cliff. Cruel words from friends hurt more than any scrape she might get crawling through a tight cave passage.

She whooshed through the siphon as if on a waterpark ride, and popped up on the other side barely out of breath. "That was great," she announced, then ducked chin-deep into the water when she saw there was a man with Sydney and Lynne.

"Who are you? Where's my daddy?" When they reached their hands out to pull Kate in, she said, "Wait, I have to tug it three times first."

"We know," Mark said. "Here, let us help you."

"No. I can do it." She yanked on the webbing to give her signal. "Okay, they know I'm safe now. Can I go again? That was fun!"

"Sorry, we have to get you warm and let the others through," Mark said, chuckling and shaking his head.

"Okay. But can you get me a blanket like they have before I

get out of the water? I kind of don't have many clothes on," Kate said primly. She untied the webbing then made Mark turn his back while she wound herself up in the blanket. "Where's my dad? Wait'll he sees what I did. Mom's coming through last, after Nicole, Melissa, and Gabby. Nicole has a hurt arm. And Gabby doesn't want to swim through at all."

"Your father's on his way. He sure is going to be happy to see you. My name is Chris. There are more rescuers on the way so we can help Nicole take care of her arm, and help the rest of your friends out." Chris checked Kate for injuries, which gave her uncontrollable giggles. Her laughter rang out happily through the cave.

The phone rang and Chris grabbed it. "Resurgence Team. Yes, Ernie, there are three people through the siphon so far; Sydney, Lynne, and little Kate." She quickly amended her last words when she saw Kate's indignant look, "Excuse me, and Kate. They say the other four women inside are planning to swim through, too. One woman has an arm injury, and one might need some special assistance with the swim. Max should be arriving any second; in fact, I think I can hear them now. We'll put him on the moment he gets here to give you an update."

Max charged through the cave, yelling over his shoulder to the others to keep up. He'd been with Ernie when the news arrived over the phone that one of the women had made it through the siphon. He grabbed the diver and three cavers to return to the siphon immediately. Ernie would give the orders to Ashby to stop blasting, and concentrate the rescue on the siphon.

On the other side of the siphon, Nicole shivered at the thought of submerging herself in that frigid water. Her arm hurt terribly. She consoled herself that the cold water would have an anesthetic effect on her pain. If only she could numb her brain as well.

She'd have to think of the water as her friend. It would help her through and at least she wouldn't have to pull herself against anything. It certainly couldn't be any worse than the breakdown she'd had to navigate through, not once, but three times. Sumps and siphons weren't completely alien to her; she'd done a couple of short duck-unders in cave stream passages before, and she was a competent swimmer. The fact that three of her teammates had been successful was also extremely encouraging. Although she felt frustrated by her arm, she was quietly proud that it hadn't prevented her from continuing to co-lead the trip or from overcoming all the other obstacles they'd faced. Just this one more hurdle to go.

"I won't be able to take these coveralls off, you know," Nicole said to Danielle. And actually, I'm kind of glad because I get chilled so easily. I'll just have to get Sydney and Lynne to warm me up in one of the hypothermia blankets when I get through. Could you give me a hand with this harness?" Nicole fished it out of her pack so Danielle could help her with the buckles.

As soon as she was ready, Nicole gave a thumbs up to the remaining women and was slowly lowered into the current. She held on long enough to ensure control over her descent with her uninjured hand, then disappeared shouting, "*Carpe diem!*"

They waited.

And waited.

Danielle began to worry. Shouldn't she be feeling Nicole's three tugs by now? Was she just imagining strange vibrations traveling through the webbing into her listening hands? Her heart flip-flopped. Something was wrong. Perhaps since Nicole was limited to one hand, it was taking her longer. Or maybe she had gotten through and forgotten to give the signals. No. Nicole was too conscientious. Something was wrong!

Shouting to Gabby and Melissa, "Nicole's in trouble! I'll come back for you." Danielle thrust part of the webbing into Melissa's hands, switched on her helmet light, and plunged into the water, coveralls and all.

The webbing slithered through her hands as she spun through the tunnel, her light useless in the muddy water. She bumped into Nicole. Why wasn't she moving? Holding tightly to their life-line with one hand, Danielle let the current carry her over Nicole until they were side by side in the narrow fissure. There was just enough room for the two of them. Danielle felt frantically for what was holding Nicole. The gear loop on the back of her harness had snagged on a sharp rock jutting out from the wall. Nicole had twisted and turned, but wasn't able to reach around with her good hand to free herself. Danielle yanked the loop off the rock and

Nicole was swept away.

Danielle followed, praying that they would both have enough breath to make it to the end. Red dots danced behind her eyes and there was a distant humming in her ears. She wondered if drowning would be painless as freezing to death was supposed to be.

Above her, there were lights. Was she dead, she wondered? She felt herself being lifted up, and stared with awe into the face of her beloved Max.

Max and his team had arrived just as Nicole and Danielle emerged. Chris was in the water pulling Nicole to safety. Lynne yelled out to her to be careful of Nicole's injured arm. Max released Kate from a bear hug and yelling, jumped in to yank Danielle out by the collar of her coveralls. He wept as she sucked in great gulps of air.

Taking a blanket from one of the rescuers, he wrapped Danielle up in it, almost crushing her with his embrace. Danielle managed a weak smile at Kate, and was relieved to see that Nicole, Lynne, and Sydney were being well tended to. She was especially glad to see that Nicole had survived her underwater ordeal.

The diver was already suited up and in the water, and at Danielle's orders gave the webbing three good, hard tugs. He paused, then gave it another three to let the remaining two women know that both Danielle and Nicole were safely through. He would use the webbing to pull himself through, trailing a rope to make the second trip easier. Pickets and stemples wouldn't be necessary now.

Chris changed Nicole's soggy bandages and remarked at the neatness of the stitches. "Who did the handiwork on Nicole?"

"I did," Lynne said.

"Great work."

Nicole agreed, "That's one cool lady." The other women laughed at their private joke.

Nicole studied the people around her. She had been to the edge of life and teetered at its brink. Now she figured she had nothing to fear when her time came. It just hadn't been her time yet. Danielle looked at her knowingly. They'd been there together. The experience just made life all the sweeter.

"I've got to get Gabby and Melissa out. I promised them I'd

come back," Danielle said, weakly pushing herself away from Max and Kate. "I've got to go back in."

"Whoa!" Max said. "That's the diver's job, Danielle. He's already on his way. You stay here and give yourself a chance to recover. We won't leave until everyone has made it out."

On the other side, Melissa said to Gabby, "You see? I told you they'd make it. I just felt three tugs, and then three more; so that means they're both through. C'mon now, you're next, my friend."

"No. Wait. You saw Danielle's face before she went in. Something went wrong with Nicole," Gabby said.

Melissa reminded her sternly, "But we got the signal, twice. That was to let us know they made it. You have to go. Now."

Gabby gulped, "I know, Melissa. I wish I could. But I don't think I can hold my breath that long. I've been trying, really I have. Each time one of us went through, I would pretend it was me, and try to hold my breath until the three tugs came. But each time I had to cheat and take a breath early."

"Well, you have to realize that it probably took them a few minutes to catch their breath before they could give the signal, so they didn't have to hold it as long as it seems. Kate did it, and Nicole did it with an injured arm. C'mon Gabby. Hey, it can't be any harder than having a baby. You've done that." She sympathized with Gabby's feelings, but the longer they stood there talking about it, the longer it would take to get out. She was desperate to go, but she knew she would have to see Gabby through first.

"I know, but this is different," Gabby said. She searched the cave walls as if expecting a magic door to suddenly appear. A door that would swing open and allow her to walk through to the warm, sunlit world outside. Or perhaps if she just clicked her muddy heels together three times and recited, "There's no place like home," she might be transported out of this dark place. "Danielle said she would come back and get us. We have to wait for her. We have to do what she says. Besides, this is nothing like having a baby."

"Do you really think she could swim against that current? And even if she could, why make her? Let's do this before she has to risk her life a second time. This isn't that different from labor if you think about it, Gabby. When it's time to have that baby, you have no choice. You have to go through the labor, right? Well, we have no choice here either. If we don't do this, we'll either freeze to death or starve. Just jump on in there and go." Melissa put a hand on Gabby's arm. "I'll be right behind you. Don't you want to see your kid and your husband? I'm sure they're waiting out there for you. Besides, you have some important pictures to develop. C'mon."

Gabby decided it was time she got hold of herself. She pulled down the zipper of her coveralls. If not for her sake, she had to do it for Danielle and Melissa. She sure didn't want Danielle to have to swim through that thing again. And she knew Melissa well enough by now to know that she wouldn't go until Gabby took the plunge. Well, shoot. She'd just do it and think about it afterwards. Maybe this would give her the courage to do some other things in her life that she'd been putting off.

Melissa grinned approvingly as Gabby pulled the webbing up out of the water. "Now you're cookin'. Did you wrap your camera up watertight?" Gabby nodded.

"Now what?" Melissa said, looking into the ominous black water. "Gabby, there's something funny happening; it feels like more signals on the line." She stared at the dripping webbing, "One, two, three, four? Five? Six . . . wha . . ?"

Suddenly, there was a strange noise from the mouth of the siphon. They both screamed and toppled backwards in surprise.

A masked, helmeted creature was struggling against the current, trying to writhe up out of the siphon. Because they'd dropped the webbing, it disappeared back into the hole.

"Oh my God, what was that?" Gabby said.

"Gabby," whispered Melissa in dismay, "It was a diver. I saw the tank on his back. I hope he's not hurt. What have we done?" Melissa swung her flashlight back to the siphon's entrance and then shouted excitedly, "There he is. He's coming back! He's pulling himself through on the webbing. Here, let's give him a hand." They reached out and dragged the diver up onto the bank. They apologized profusely but he waved their explanations aside.

"Don't worry about it. Are you two okay? I'm Charlie and I'll help you get out. Your friends are fine. They're all waiting for you." Charlie pulled out a couple of granola bars from his

165

watertight pouch. He waited while they devoured them hungrily.

"I brought an extra air tank so you'll be able to breathe on your way through. Have you ever used scuba equipment before?"

Both women shook their heads no.

"Oh well, who's first?"

Gabby tentatively lifted a hand, "I guess I am. My name's Gabby; she's Melissa. Um, I don't know how to swim. In fact, I really don't want to do this. Isn't there another way? We heard them blasting back there."

"No ma'am; I'm afraid they said it could take days to open up the waterfall area. They've decided that this is the safest and fastest way to get you out. Your friends made it through and they're all waiting for you. Even the lady with the injured arm made it. Besides, it will be easier for you since you get to use an air tank."

"Well, I've never used one before." Thinking about the rest of her team gathered on the other side made Gabby realize how ready she was to join them. "Can I try it while we're sitting here first?"

"Sure," Charlie said, and showed her how to breathe through the mouthpiece. "You don't need to know how to swim. Just let the water carry you through. I'll be right with you. Melissa, could you please anchor this rope around that boulder over there? It'll help make the trip back for you easier since I can use an ascender on it; ascenders don't work on webbing."

Charlie and Gabby waited while Melissa tied the rope. "You're all set," she said, "and I pulled in the webbing since you're using the rope. That way you won't have to worry about getting tangled up in it.

"Thanks. Okay Gabby, when we get in the water, I'll be right with you. It'll go fast. Toward the end, it gets pretty narrow so I'll let you go first. Just breathe in and out through the mouthpiece, nice and regular. We'll be out of here in a jiffy. You have quite a crowd waiting for you on the other side. Ready?"

Gabby felt for the small fannypack where her camera and film were wrapped carefully in plastic bags. There was no way she was going to leave those precious pictures behind. They were her medals. "Ready."

She clenched the mouthpiece between her teeth and forced her breath in and out at a steady pace. They swung out into the stream and she could feel the current pulling at her, flapping her wet clothes around her legs. Her heart was pumping wildly and for a split second she wanted to change her mind, to fight the current, and claw her way back to Melissa.

Then, a small voice inside her said, "Now's your chance. Stick with it and let it happen. Breathe in, breathe out. Go!"

The moment she relaxed, the current took her. What a strange feeling. No up or down, just darkness. Flying through liquid space. She opened her eyes and saw blackness. She heard a dull clank as her tank hit a wall. She was doing it. She was alive. She kept thinking, I wish I could take a picture of this.

Melissa was all alone now. The water seemed to be singing to her in low, guttural tones. You sound like an old bear gargling, she mocked it back silently. You don't scare me. She stood erect, foot tapping, arms folded across her chest and stared back at its black, unwinking eye.

Fear and utter loneliness circled her like two hungry wolves. She imagined a pair of yellow eyes watching her from behind, waiting for her to weaken and give in. The thudbeat of her heart kept its steady tempo. You'll never get me, she thought. My heart is beating like a drum. Drumming my song of strength. I take your challenge into my veins and transform it into courage. "I'm strong," she said out loud.

"I don't need any air tank. And I'm not waiting for any diver, either. Aieeeeee!" she whooped and shoved off the bank. Her head swam with images of all the earth's water-loving creatures: otters, seals and dolphins, cormorants, manatees. The water would deliver her back to land where her feet would dance again through sunny green fields of grass and soft warm carpets of pine needles. The stream sang through her hair as she shot through the opening, and narrowly missed colliding with the diver.

Charlie twisted out of the way as he saw two boots heading straight for his masked face. "Whoa!" he bubbled into his mouthpiece. He swerved around to help her, but she was already pulling up onto the bank to be blanketed like the others.

"Sorry, Charlie. I just couldn't wait," Melissa croaked, her voice nearly gone from the exertions of the past few days.

"Hey, sisters. We're all here. Can you believe it?"

"I can," Max said. He cranked the phone to give Ernie the best possible news. He watched the women hug and hold each other, with the profound feeling of having witnessed a miracle. "Ernie, they're all out. All seven. Chris is checking Melissa now and the way she came spitting out of that thing, I imagine she's going to check out in fine shape. Charlie's gone in with a helper to retrieve their gear. After the women have a little more time to recover, we'll start making our way out."

Ernie's voice caught for a moment as he replied, "I already talked to Ashby and the Dynamite Team. They've packed up and are on their way out. We'll send as much help as you need. I know you'll be anxious to get home and get some sleep."

"Sleep?" said Max, grinning at Danielle, "Yeah, that too. Have you been able to let the family members know that everyone's out? Aren't most of them waiting in the tent?"

"They know," Ernie said. "I'm surprised you couldn't hear their cheers. "Hang on a minute. There's someone who just walked up that wants to talk to Danielle. Can she get to the phone?"

"Sure," Max said, one eyebrow lifted quizzically. He handed Danielle the phone, keeping one arm around her.

"Is this the leader of the cave women?" Ashby said.

"One of them," Danielle said, looking at Nicole. "Who's this?"

Max whispered that it was the dynamiter, Ashby Thompson.

"I jes wanted to hear your voice and make sure you and all the other folks was safe and sound. And, your little girl, what's her name?"

"Kate. And she's not so little, to tell you the truth," Danielle said, smiling at Kate. "Thank you, Mr. Thompson, for all your efforts. I'm glad you won't have to blast anymore, though."

"You kin call me Ashby. I'm glad too. This is a right purty ol' cave. Even if she was being stubborn. Well, I saved Miss Kate a piece of apple pie. You just tell her to look for me when she reaches daylight, and we'll have a regular little picnic. And the rest of us'll crack open the mason jar I've got stashed in my truck and have us a toast. Deal?"

"Deal," Danielle said, leaning tiredly against Max's shoulder. She handed him back the phone, and looked around at the

others. "I want to thank every one of you for your help. For being here, and getting the tank to Gabby. I . . ." She began to cry.

Their attention was suddenly drawn to some arriving rescuers who were coming to help carry out gear and equipment. One of them was twirling something red around his finger as he casually loped toward them.

"These belong to anyone?" he said.

"Oh my God," groaned Lynne, her cheeks turning pink.

"Mom? What is it?" Kate said, pulling on Danielle's sleeve.

"Sssh, it's Lynne's panties."

Lynne lunged forward, her movements impeded by the blanket, then snatched the torn red lingerie out of his hands. "I'll take those, thank you," she said haughtily and grabbed Gabby by the arm. "Why don't you take your picture so we can go home?"

Gabby lined up her teammates. "Wait," Melissa said, "You have to be in this picture, Gabby. It's your last shot, isn't it? You have to be in it. Hey—you—you that found the underwear. You take the picture." Everyone chuckled as he sheepishly accepted the camera and listened politely to Gabby's strict instructions.

Smiles lit up their faces. The women were living portraits of pride. Satisfaction glowed in their eyes, intensified with the ecstasy of accomplishing what had seemed impossible. When the flash went off, it illuminated the room in a blaze of victory. Gabby quickly took her camera back and wrapped it for their final steps through the cave.

As the remaining gear was collected, Chris and Mark offered to carry Nicole out, knowing she must be exhausted from her injury and underwater close-call.

"I walked in," Nicole said, "I walk out. Thanks, but I'm fine. Fine as frog hair."

"Is that Latin, too Nicole?" Kate said.

"Well, no, but this is: *Annuit coeptis.*" With her chin slightly raised, she took her place among the women, and whispered to Kate, "God has smiled on our undertakings."

"Undertakings? I like that one, Nicole."

Max moved forward to lead them out of the cave, then stopped and looked at Danielle. "Here," he said, "You lead out. We'll follow." He gave an almost imperceptible bow and stepped aside.

Epilogue

In the photo, the seven women look exhausted but happy. Their faces glow as if illuminated from within, rather than by the camera's flash. Water droplets on the dark cave walls pick up the light to form a shimmering backdrop for the victorious crew.

Kate left the rest of the mail in the mailbox and ran into the house, waving the magazine high in the air.

"Mom! Daddy! Look what's on the cover of the *NSS News*!"